ALTAR CALL

I COME BOLDLY TO YOUR THRONE OF GRACE

VOL. 2

BY

Gwarmekia Sturdivant

ISBN: 978-1-7337133-0-6

Table of Contents

Dedication

This book is dedicated to everyone who sometimes feel misunderstood, unloved, or alone. I just want to remind you that God sees you, God knows you, God loves you, and you are not alone. Hold your head up and walk in His Love.

Acknowledgments

Thank You Lord for providing me with the words to write to create books that are pleasing to you, and stories that will reach your people right where they are. Thank you for using me for your glory.

Introduction

Finding my way back to you seems difficult. I feel as though I am bearing this walk alone, no one to help me through it. But, You, are always available at all times with a listening ear to attentively hear me, and your arms are opened wide to freely embrace me. There were times I talked myself out of your presence only because I didn't feel good enough to stand there beside you. But, today, I let all of that doubt go, and I say goodbye to all of the things that would separate us. I feel stronger than I've ever been. I am learning to understand my purpose through the trials. I learn my true beauty as the fire refines me and purges me of everything that keeps me from shining bright. As I continue to grow, I will continue to seek You for more direction, more communication between the two of us, and more work for me to do towards the up-building of Your Kingdom. I know that You don't need me because there are so many others You could use. Thanks for using me...

Chapter 1

The Woman in You

The Woman in You
He said, "I want to love you like Christ loves the church."
"Hmmm?"
But soon you figured out that this man did not even know Christ.

He didn't even know what Love was and had not been to the church
since his youth.
You figured out that he cannot Love like Christ because he does not
know Christ.
This man could only empty you by using vain words to attempt to fill
you up.
Your cup runneth over with compliments but empty with real love.

Deep down inside you could only be filled by God's love and His
replenishing power.
Only God can mend a broken heart.
Only God can remove those unmovable mountains that stand tall.

So, you cry aloud, "Fill every void in me oh God," because you know
that you cannot do this on your own.
God will step in and fill every void in due time.
His timing is perfect timing.
Dare not rush His hand and dare not deface his work.
Once the job is done;
Once he has renewed you;
Once you are restored;

It's going to take the Woman in you to hold on tight to God's unchanging hand.
It's going to take the Woman in you to turn away from the Christ "wannabe" who claims to love you.
It's going to take the Woman in you and Christ's word to know that the circle of chains and bondage that will attempt to come back can stay broken only if the Woman in you will take a stand.

Where is the Woman in you?
Who is the Woman in you?
Can you find her?
Do you know her?

Are you looking for a man to justify her and who she is?
Get to know her and understand every being of her.
She deserves to be known and to be first loved by Christ
And second, loved by you.
She desires it and craves it.

So, before you meet a man, learn the Woman in you,
Date her and make love to her
And know love her so deeply that she identifies the lies,
And faces them with the truth.
Learn who she is;

Learn the Woman in You!

Chapter 2

Love Conquers All

It's so easy to give up nowadays because love is not as authentic as it used to be. Nobody forgives, everyone is throwing in the towel due to lack of love. When you love someone, you should love through the worst times the most because that is when the devil is attacking and trying hard to break your relationship or friendship. He destroys anything that looks good. If it looks like love, he is on his way to instill hate. He is an invisible instigator. Anytime there is a fight, he is right there laughing in the midst of it because he thinks it's cute. He knows that the more people fight; it will more than likely cause a broken relationship or a split friendship. But what he doesn't know is that God is the author and finisher, and what he put together, not even the tempter can destroy it.

Chauncey has been faithful to his wife for six years. They dated for two years and have been married for four. They have no children; due to their busy lifestyle, they don't even have a pet. Chauncey works as a surgeon at Oakdale Medical Hospital. He has been excelling and making a name for himself since college. He's one of the best surgeons in his district, and very well known in other states. Chauncey has one of the sweetest hearts you could ever come across. He has character, he walks with dignity, and he is an easy-going fellow. He is the type that remained calm in difficult situations, and instead of money making him arrogant, he grows humble. He met his wife Denise while out shopping for his mother's birthday gift. He was the type that never approached women because of his shy and bashful demeanor. As soon as he walked in Macy's, he saw her very beautiful smile first and then he looked at the way she carried herself. He thought to himself, and then he walked closer to see her up close. She was natural. She did not wear make-up and did not need extensions due to her long wavy hair. Her lips were shaped like hearts, her body was shaped like the figure eight, and she had nice toes. She was conversing with an older lady, and the lady must have said something hilarious because Denise couldn't stop laughing. When she composed herself, she glanced over, and Chauncey was standing there. He walked up to her, and she began to blush. She saw cute guys enter and exit the department store all the time, but she was never interested in anybody. Those guys didn't catch her eye like Chauncey did. There was something in Chauncey's eye that gave her a notification of peace and safety. He said, "Hello, I need some help." He looked down at his feet because he began to feel shy again. She smiled because she thought it was so adorable. She responded, "What may I assist you with sir?" Chauncey began to get tongue-tied and couldn't seem to open his mouth. "Um, well, um, I am looking for something for my mom. Her birthday is tomorrow, and I wanted something special for her." He was very nervous. She grabbed his arm and walked with him over to the perfume counter. "How old is your mom going to be?" She asked questions so that she would be able to serve him a little better. "What type of things do you think she would she like? Do you think she would prefer perfume, clothing, or something for the house?" He was ready to talk, but still nervous at the same time. "Well, she is about to be seventy. But she does not look like she's seventy, nor does she act like a seventy-year-old might. She looks about fifty, and she acts like she is thirty. She is very hip, and she still got it." He smiled proudly. "So, she is like one of those sexy, laid-back moms, huh?" They both smiled at each other. He looked down at his feet again and opened his mouth and hesitated before speaking. "Look, I don't know if you have a boyfriend or anything, but..." "I don't," she interrupted before he could finish. They both smiled, and he said, "are you available to go out next weekend?" He was still nervous. "I'd be delighted to go out with you." Denise hadn't been involved with anyone since her last boyfriend who had an anger problem. He was very abusive and a little crazy. But the last time she was in love with anyone was with her boyfriend in college. She hasn't seen or heard from him since college. She was so excited because most guys are intimidated by her beauty and class that they won't come near her. Although Chauncey was nervous, he stepped up to her and asked her out. That impressed her and made her glow a little. She gave him her number and said, "I will be expecting your call."

He walked away smiling and trying to figure out where he could take a beautiful, classy woman to have some fun.

The first date was amazing. He picked her up at five in his Avalanche, and they were on their way. He asked her about different restaurants and places that may be nice to dine in. But he already had everything prepared. He made small conversations just to keep her from guessing what they were going to do that evening. She really didn't know where they were going, but he planned a nice evening for her. He sliced strawberries, plums, and mango. He had pecans, walnuts, and honey roasted peanuts. He also had little sandwiches that he made himself and sliced them really neat. He made blackberry lemonade with honey early that morning and made sure it was chilled by the time they were ready to go. They pulled up to a beautiful park, and she couldn't stop smiling. He got out of the car, went around to her side and opened her door and helped her out. He opened the back door afterward and grabbed the picnic basket and a blanket to sit on. He also had a pillow for her just in case the ground was too hard for her. She blushed and started to cover her mouth, but he grabbed her hand. He led her to a nice spot to sit and while he sat everything up, she looked around admiring the beautiful green trees with the wind blowing through the leaves; she looked at the swan and geese in the clear water. Her smile began to widen. After spreading out the blanket, he grabbed her hand and led her to the pillow. "You can sit here if you want." He took her shoes off and put them aside. He grabbed a couple of wet naps so that they can sanitize their hands. She was so shocked at how he planned everything without missing a beat. He didn't miss a step; he was on point with every single thought. "This is so beautiful Chauncey. I have never been on a picnic before." He smiled at her and said "I haven't either. I always wanted to go on one with the right person. The first thing I could think of when you said yes to go out with me was a picnic." Chauncey was so sincere, and they were both glowing. He had little paper plates and began to serve her some fruit and nuts. He gave her half of a sandwich so that he wouldn't offend her. He didn't want to overcrowd her plate. She looked at him and said, "I am not afraid to eat, in fact, I will take a little more fruit and the other half of that sandwich." He chuckled, and they both began to laugh. He liked her sense of humor and how she could make him laugh. They ate and watched the sunset, and they walked around the park a little bit to talk. They began seeing each other every week and then every few days, and then they felt they couldn't go without seeing each other. Months went by, and everything flowed smoothly. They grew fond of each other and fell madly in love by six months. They did not have sexual intercourse; they wanted to wait until marriage before they made it to that step. Chauncey started looking around for rings and a new home. He did a few things without her knowing because he wanted her to be surprised. He always loved seeing her face when he did something for her. He enjoyed making her happy and making her smile. It wasn't hard to make her smile after going through such a bad relationship in previous years. She enjoyed the person that he is and how he was always into her. He found the perfect ring after searching for a month. He was not sure on how to propose so he kept the ring for another month until he could think of how to ask. He was always coming up with something amazing to do for her. Finally, he decided to take her back to the park where they had their first date. By this time, it was a little cold outside, and he had a cute little plan. He picked her up and talked to her about vacations. He wanted to know where she would like to go if she could get away for a few days. He was planning the honeymoon and hadn't even proposed yet. But he was always thinking ahead so that he could make her happy. She told him, "I would like to go to Hawaii or Rio." They talked about both and what it would be like to see the ocean and walk on the sandy beaches. They pulled up to the park, and he did what a gentleman usually would do; he got out of the car and went to the passenger side and opened her door for her. He held her hand and led her to the same area where they had their first picnic. Someone seemed to have set up everything for him. There were rose petals, candles, and balloons around the picnic area. Everything was shaped like hearts. He also hired a photographer to snap some shots of the two while they were there. He wanted to capture every moment of surprise and give it to her later. Chauncey said to her, "looks like somebody may be in love." She looked around to see where the people were who could have possibly done this and just left it there. "It looks so beautiful; I wonder where they could be." Chauncey walked over to where everything was set up and said to her, "they are here." She said to him, "Why are you over here spoiling someone else's surprise?" He looked at her, got down on one knee and smiled. "Come here for a second and answer me this. Will you marry me?" Tears rolled down her cheeks, and she smiled at him. "You are always up to something." She began to get speechless like always. He began to get just a little frightened because she did not give an answer yet. He asked again, "will you marry me? I love you and want to be with you, but if you..." She interrupted him, "Yes. I will marry you today if you want to." He put the ring on her finger, and they both smiled and kissed each other like there was no tomorrow. He held her close, and she squeezed him tight. "I love you girl." He couldn't stop looking at his woman.

A simple wedding was planned. They wanted it to be private and sweet. There were only about ten people there in all. It was a day to remember.

He finally showed her two of the homes that he thought about getting but left it up to her to make the final choice. She loved them both, and they decided to go with the home that was more kid-friendly. He didn't blow her mind every single day with something spectacular, but he tried to make every day count. He wrote little letters and love notes and placed them by the bed so that when she awakens out of her sleep, she would have a smile on her face. He wanted her days to start off with love and to end with love. Little notes were left on the fridge and also on her vanity. He would even place little gifts in the car or in the walk-in closet. He was always kind and sweet to her and always wanted her to know that he cared for her. He always put God first and his wife second.

As the years rushed by, things started to change. Chauncey remained the same, but Denise started to wonder. He had a feeling she was having an affair but had no proof. He tried very hard to erase those thoughts and tried his best to never let his mind go to that place again. But those suspicious thoughts kept creeping back. "What should I do God? I love my wife; I would do anything for her. Should I hire someone to follow her? I trust you, God, please reveal every hidden thing in my marriage; bring everything to the surface." Denise walked in the kitchen, "hey baby, what are you cooking?" She didn't give Chauncey a kiss, and she didn't wait for a reply. She grabbed something to drink and kept going. She walked to their bedroom and opened her laptop. "You've got mail," her computer spoke aloud. "I wonder if this is Darnell." She got all excited, it was Darnell. Darnell and Denise go way back to her freshman year of college. He was her first, and she was his. They recently reconnected after all these years. Everything started off innocent, but it seemed to get a little serious after they started speaking on the past. Darnell always asked, "Did you miss me?" And Denise always responded, "a little bit." They would always flirt back and forth, and it started to become serious. She wanted to do what was right, but she couldn't stop thinking about the way Darnell used to hold her and kiss her. He did everything the way she liked. He spoiled her, showed her love and affection, and made love to her passionately. She thought he was the one for her and he thought the same. He left after freshman year of college and decided to go to a two-year college closer to home. They kept in touch for a while, but school got in the way, and they both had to stay focused. But here they are, together again at last. Oh, how she missed him. Chauncey came up the stairs. "Baby, what are you doing?" With one push of a button, the screen went to Neiman Marcus. "Oh, those are hot, aren't they?" She asked Chauncey. "Yeah, I like those. How much are they?" "They are only $175," she answered. "You can't find any a little cheaper than that, like at Sears, or Dillard's or something? Have you looked at any sales that may have something similar to those?" he asked while making his way to the closet. "Well this is real leather, and I am not asking you to buy them for me. I can get them myself." She started thinking to herself, and the devil also helped her remember that Darnell would never ask how much something cost. He would just go get it for her if he knew that is what she desired. Darnell would buy her things and spoil her and made sure that she would have the things she wanted. She started to reminisce about Darnell again. It seemed as though he still had a piece of her heart. She started to feel like she made a mistake, and that's how her love affair began. "Baby, I finished cooking, are you ready to eat?" Chauncey had changed his clothes and decided to put on something a little more comfortable to lounge in. The football game was coming on soon, and he wanted to eat with his wife first. Denise answered quickly, "I'm on my way downstairs." She got back on the other page to let Darnell know that she wanted to see him on Friday at 7pm. Chauncey will have a few friends over for one of the big games, and she will be able to be free for a couple of hours.

Denise went downstairs to eat with her hubby. He fixed her plate and had it on the table already. "How was your day, boo?" Chauncey tried to spark a conversation with his wife just to see how she was doing. "It was good baby." She answered every question promptly without going into detail. The first few years of their marriage were awesome. She couldn't stay away from him. She was very clingy to him and always wanted to talk to him. This year was different, Darnell was back in her life and found a way to get to her heart. They have been chatting and emailing each other and longing to have another encounter with each other. Denise wanted to meet up with Darnell plenty of times before, but Darnell's job has him traveling back and forth out of town. But now, they will be able to see each other face to face. The anticipation of seeing her old lover is getting her so excited that she cannot even eat her dinner. Chauncey has been watching her at the table, she has not put anything in her mouth. She is smiling and twirling her fork through the food. He made her favorite meal, and she did not taste any of it. His suspicions are brewing on the inside of his mind. There is something up, but he does not know what it is or what it could be. What can he really say at this point? It's way too early for him to assume anything. "Sweetie, how's your food?" He asked, waiting and watching his wife. Her eyes were glowing, she seemed to have been trying to hide her smile but have a weird smirk on her face. "Um, Um," she quickly stuffed some of the steamed veggies in her mouth and said, "It's very delicious baby." She looked up at him, and he glanced at her, and then over at the clock. It was time for the game to come on. He went to the kitchen and cleaned the dishes that were there and made sure the kitchen was neat before watching the game. He grabbed a couple of mango juices out of the fridge and headed to the living area. He sat down in his favorite chair and reclined all the way back. Denise decided to throw her food away and get back upstairs on the internet. She checked her email again, and Darnell wrote another message. "I miss you so much, can't wait to see you Friday." She smiled as she walked to the closet to figure out what she would wear. " Maybe I should wear some jeans and a nice little top showing him my lil figure. Or maybe a nice fitted black dress, shoulders out, hair up, red lipstick, coach shoes, coach bag, and gold jewelry. I don't know, maybe I am doing too much. This is our first time seeing each other in a while. I should just dress casual, psych! I am about to see my first love and show him what he has been missing out on all these years." She walked over to the dresser to find some pajamas. All the excitement has tired her out. It was time for some much-deserved shut eye. She believed in getting her eight hours of beauty rest. Looking good was very important to her. After her shower, she put her cleansing mask on, and let it sit for fifteen minutes. While she let it sink into her pores, she decided to watch a little television. "My Wife and Kids are on, oh yeah. Damon Wayans is such a cutie." By the middle of the show, she figured it was high time to peel her mask off. Afterwards, she flossed and brushed her teeth. Ready for bed, she unplugged everything and finally got into bed and rested her head on her pillow. She was out in about five minutes. Chauncey came up the stairs to check on his wife as usual. He kissed her gently on the forehead and covered her with a little blanket. He then returned back down stairs to finish watching the game. His team won the game, so of course, the team will be going to the Super bowl. Chauncey was ecstatic. He jumped in the shower, got into bed and wrapped his arms around his wife. "Stop it, baby, I'm too tired," Denise whispered softly. He turned over, and at first, he felt a negative spirit try to come over him. But he decided to pray to God and thank God for everything that he has done for him, and God put joy in His heart. He had a sweet sleep that night.

It was morning, and the sun was shining on his face. He got out of bed, got ready for work and went to fix breakfast as usual. By the time she got down stairs, she had beaten him to the stove and made his favorite. She had prepared him a cheese omelet with onions, ham, peppers, and bacon. "Dang baby, what did I do to deserve this?" He was a little surprised considering that last night she wasn't giving off a good vibe. "I just wanted to say I'm sorry, I had a lot on my mind last night. But I am good now." She gave him a big hug after her apology, and she headed upstairs to put on her moisturizers and her eye cream. She put her suit on, and she was ready to head out for work. She had a lot of clients. She was great with helping people gain confidence about their skin and their appearance. She gave4 them helpful tips, and always succeeded in helping them achieve their goals of becoming beautiful and confident. Denise had a few male clients, but most of them were women. While she was helping one client, a male came up behind her and said, "Guess who?" She knew that it couldn't be Chauncey, he had to work. "Darnell? What are you doing here?" She told him where she worked, never expecting that he would show up. "I just wanted to see you. I was hoping I could take you to lunch if you had time." "I do have time after this client," she answered. Her client was very observant. She noticed that Denise had a wedding ring on and that the young man who was standing there did not. "I will be finished in about five minutes, so just walk around the store a little and meet me back over here." As Darnell walked away, the client said to her, "Be careful sweetie. Drink waters out of thine own cistern and running waters out of thine own well." Denise did not know what that statement meant, but it was time for her to go, so she cleaned up her station and headed out. When she got to the car and saw Darnell, she couldn't stop smiling. "Darnell, I cannot believe that you came up here. You look handsome as you always have." She had a glow on her face, she was excited. He said to her, "You still have that banging body that I love so much." The devil was all up in his eyes. All he had was lust on his mind. He saw her legs and her pretty skin, and he was ready to rip those clothes off of her. "So, what are we going to eat?" She looked into his eyes, "Well I was thinking, either Red Lobster, or some kind of sushi place. I love seafood," he said. "Then after we eat, I want to take you shopping, you pick out what you want. I will pay for it. "She was all giddy like a little girl. She knew that he would spoil her once he came back into her life. It's not like Chauncey wouldn't spoil her, he just likes to be reasonable and conservative with money. Which is very smart, but sometimes, you should do something unexpected for the one you love every now and again. At least that's how Denise thought it should have been. Darnell made sure to give her what she wanted, after all, he knew that he wanted something in return. He said, "what did you miss most about me?" "Well, I missed your scent, I love the way you used to smell. Curve, that is the cologne you used to always wear." "I still do." She smiled, "what have you been up to? Why don't you have a wife with your fine self?" Asking that question only gave him all the more reason to play the pity me role. He said to her with the look of desperate longing, "All I want is you." She smiled so hard from ear to ear. She couldn't believe that he still wanted her. Her mind is racing with thoughts now. "What if I am supposed to be with Darnell instead of Chauncey? I've always been in love with him; maybe I am supposed to be with him." Her mind started playing tricks on her.

As soon as they arrived at the restaurant, he treated her like a real princess. He opened the door, pulled out the chair, this dude even remembers what type of food she likes and ordered for her. She was in a deep gaze as they talked and waited on their food. In walked some of her friends. They noticed her, but she didn't notice them. He looked familiar to them, but they couldn't put their finger on it at the right moment. It was obvious that Denise was into this guy. But whoever this guy is, he is not her husband. The waiter, a tall, handsome young man, brought drinks to the table. He looked at Denise's ring, and he noticed Darnell didn't have on a ring. He looked directly at Denise and made eye contact with her. He then walked away from the table. "Are we still meeting up tomorrow?" she asked. "Yes, I hope so. I do want to see you while I am here. We can do whatever you want to do." Denise did not know exactly what to say. The waiter was on his way with the food. She said to Darnell, "I need to wash my hands really quick, I will be right back." Darnell just smiled. He had his eyes on her body the entire time. She looked back at him once she started walking away. She was flattered at the way he looked at her. While she walked away, he watched her booty the way it bounced and jiggled. He admired her thighs; they were so juicy and thick. Darnell's co-pilot could not wait to touch and feel her insides. He sat there and thought of all the things that he wanted to do, how he could please her and make her want more of him. It's not like Chauncey never told her she was beautiful. She wanted to be looked at by the eyes of a man who wanted to rip her clothes off. Once she got in the restroom, two of her friends entered right behind her. "Hey Denise, how are you doing? Yeah, how are you?" asked Stacey and Marvis. Shocked to see them there and feeling a little ashamed on the inside, she answered, "I'm doing well." "So, who are you with again? Because that is not Chauncey at the table," asked Stacey. "He looks very familiar, but I can't remember quite clear." Marvis wanted to say a little more, but Stacey stopped her. Marvis knew that Chauncey was a great husband and that he did not deserve to be treated disrespectfully. But she cannot tell Denise what to do, after all, Denise is a grown woman that will have to learn on her own. While Denise stood there nervous, she grew speechless. She looked as if guilt was sitting in her throat and choking to come out of her. "We are going to go and finish up our meal, it was nice seeing you." Stacey and Marvis said and started to exit the facilities. Denise stood there, and took three deep long breaths, and then made her exit. She walked back to the table in contempt. She sat down and slowly looked up at him. After the encounter in the ladies' room, she wanted to back out of future plans with Darnell. She said, "Look, maybe we shouldn't see each other tomorrow. I am married, and I don't want to mess up." She was trying to convince herself, but it did not work because she did not convince him. He talked her into seeing him anyway. He said, "We can just go to the park. It will be innocent. What's wrong with two friends seeing each other and reminiscing? What's the harm in that? I will not make you do anything you do not want to do." She knew deep down inside that she wanted to see her long lost love. It did not look right for her to see him, but what was the harm in it? She smiled and said, "Yeah, we can go to the park." He interrupted. "But they do have this new movie coming out, and we can see it in the daytime if you want." He was trying to be slick once again, knowing that during the movie, it will be very dark. He wanted her in the dark anyway; all to himself. The mood would be just right. She told him, "The movies will be fine." They ate their food and got ready to go on a shopping spree. He bought her a few things. She didn't want to pick out too much stuff. But she did end up getting those boots she wanted from Neiman Marcus that her husband thought was

25

too expensive. After shopping, they loaded up his car. His black four-door Porsche made her feel like she was the first lady. He treated her like she was so important to him. As they drove back to her car, they glanced at each other periodically. Once they pulled up to her vehicle, he actually turned the car off to help her out of her car and to get her bags inside of her car. And of course, a long, enticing hug. "I will see you, tomorrow right?" He whispered as he rubbed her back a little. "Yes." Denise smiled and inhaled a big gasp of air and slowly let it exit her full lips. They separated themselves and finally entered their own vehicle. She drove off thinking of Darnell and how he spoils her rotten. Then after about five minutes, she began to compare her husband and Darnell to each other. Denise feels confused. "Have I married the wrong man? What if I was supposed to wait a little longer?" When she arrived home, Chauncey was not there. She began to get the bags out and hurry up stairs to put everything away where nothing could be suspected by Chauncey. She put her new lingerie, jewelry, shoes, and clothes in places that Chauncey never would look. She then threw all the shopping bags away and emptied the garbage. When Chauncey walked into the house, he smelled an aroma that was new to his nostrils. Denise cooked dinner. She usually would stay away from the kitchen. The dining room table was set up nice and neat. Chauncey sat down and smiled. He was excited to see his woman cooking and thinking of him. But he wanted to know where all of this was coming from. "Baby, I came by your job today to take you to lunch. You were not there. Where were you?" Chauncey was very curious. "Oh baby, I left a little early to do a little window shopping and to get home to cook for us." She tried so hard to make it seem like a normal day, but it was not. Darnell came to town and stirred up some trouble. She began cheating emotionally and did not know it. The tempter, disguised as Darnell, had come into her marriage to cause discord. Very clever, that tempter is. He got her right where he wanted her. While eating, she kept her eyes on her food. She was too nervous to look up at her husband's face. After only taking a few bites, she went upstairs to get ready for a shower. All that walking and entertaining her ex-flame left her exhausted. She undressed and looked in the mirror. She examined and admired her body. Pulling her hair up and pouting her lips out, she thought of how beautiful she was and how Darnell craved her. Hearing footsteps coming towards the bedroom, she hurried and jumped in the shower. Chauncey walked in the restroom and asked, "May I join you, Sweetie?" "No Baby, I am just trying to relax right now." She rejected her husband. He was not mad at her. He respected her answer and went down stairs to watch the game. She closed her eyes and imagined Darnell being in the shower with her instead. She could feel his touch, she could feel his kiss. She opened her eyes and tried to snap out of it. "Denise, you are married." The voice inside her head tried to convict her. It wasn't working. She dismissed the voice because she wanted Darnell. She missed Darnell. She got out of the shower and put on her robe. She fixed her hair and prepared for tomorrow. She was off every weekend but had to shop and runaround for her hubby's super bowl party. She sat on her bed and wrote down everything Chauncey always desired for the parties he would host. Denise was excited. She thought about everything. What she would wear to the store, what she would wear leaving the house before meeting up with Darnell, and what she would change into for their movie night. She had planned out everything from Friday morning until Friday evening. She didn't know Darnell had plans of his own and couldn't realize that he is in the process of ruining their marriage. It wouldn't be long now before she finds out. Denise went downstairs, "hey baby, I wrote out a list of things you may want for tomorrow's game; but I want you to look over it and let me know if there is anything I'm missing." Chauncey was surprised to see that she wanted to help out for the game. Glancing at the list with a smile he answered, "No baby, you aren't missing anything, and everything will be more than enough." He was so easy going, never asked for anything from his wife. He loves and trusts her so much that he wouldn't be able to detect if she is doing him wrong. He wasn't hard to please. He was very faithful and hardworking, never thought of anyone else besides his beautiful wife being by his side. Why would she want to risk all of that? Why would she sneak around on a good man when so many women are searching for a good man? He started to turn off the lights, and they headed upstairs to get some rest. He first jumped in the shower, and he sang a song while he got all the dirt off of him. After stepping out of the shower, he walked in the bedroom to hold his beautiful wife, but she wasn't available for him. She had fallen asleep, well at least that is what she portrayed to be doing. He got up to find some boxers and a t shirt and glanced over and saw those boots that they talked about lying on the floor on her side of the closet. All he could do was shake his head. Without thinking too much about anything that happened with him and her today, he decided to just close his eyes and get some rest. After all, the game is tomorrow.

It was a little cloudy that morning when she woke up and looked out of the window. But she still has to get out of the house in order to get her day started. She went into the dresser to grab her black bra and found a white tea that said 'hot stuff' on the front of it. She slipped into some sweat pants and grabbed her sneakers. Denise grabbed her purse and made sure she put the list inside so she wouldn't forget anything. Heading out of the front door, the umbrella inside the stand seemed to be waiting for her to choose it, so she did. Chauncey opened his eyes when he heard the door shut downstairs. He got out of bed to look out of the window, and he watched as his wife drove off. He put on his basketball shorts and old sneakers to cut the lawn. He kept the house looking neat and clean on the outside, he even planted flowers to give it some color when they first moved in. By the time he finished cutting the front and back yard, she was back with the groceries. He decided to trim the hedges and also cleaned the grass and debris off the back patio. She went inside and started working on the meat for the Ro-tel dip, and also put the wings in the oven. Denise cooked fried chicken, baked chicken and she also did hot wings. She bought cookies, chips, and nuts, fruit, and drinks. All the other groceries for the house she put away and made sure that everything was clean. Everything looked nice and neat and thoughtful. While her husband was still outdoors, she went upstairs to pack her bag with a couple of outfits that she might want to change into and hurried to take them downstairs to put them in the car before Chauncey could catch her. She came back inside to clean the restroom and get the living area ready so that she will be able to set up the food better. She lit candles so that the house would have that fresh smell, well at least before the game anyway. Men sometimes smell like they have been playing in the game and have only been watching it. "Hey baby," Chauncey said while walking in and looking at his beautiful wife. He walked over and attempted to give her a kiss. "Eeewww, you're sweaty, Chauncey." She smiled and still kissed him but immediately went upstairs to wash up and rest. Chauncey looked around the house and began to feel that energy that comes from watching a football game and being with his boys. He went upstairs to shower and noticed Denise asleep again. He went over and put a little blanket on her to keep her warm after turning on the air. A text came through to her phone, it was Darnell of course. Instead of Chauncey spying on her or investigating, he continued to finish up what he had planned to do before the game. He went downstairs and snuck a few wings and turned on the television getting excited. The time now was one o'clock p.m., and his boys were probably on their way. There were two games to watch tonight.

Denise opened her eyes and rolled over to grab her phone. She finally read Darnell's text. It read, "Can't wait to see you," with little hearts attached to the message. It made her smile. She immediately jumped out of bed and leaped to the closet in excitement and started to put her clothes together. She took everything in the bathroom with her so that once she jumps in and out of the shower; she can get into her outfit quickly and get out of the house. She picked out some cute black leggings with a light gray sweater and ankle boots. Meanwhile, downstairs, a few of the guys have shown up for the game. "What's up Chauncey? Thanks for having us over man, this game is about to be sick." The guys were having their man talks about the game while sneaky Denise was upstairs spraying Estee Lauder all over her. She grabbed her Louis Vuitton bag and jetted down the stairs to say hello to the guests; "Hello boys, ya'll have fun now." She quickly kissed Chauncey and said, "Alright baby, I will see you later. I love you." Chauncey kissed her back and hugged her

tight and said, "I love you too baby, and thank you for all of this."
There was a prick that quickly darted her heart. Her phone started
vibrating, and it suddenly took her mind off what the prick might
have been. She got inside of her car and started up the car and put
her music on. "Yes Avant, sing to me." She loved her some Avant
and KeKe Wyatt. She drove and sang and didn't think of anything
besides Darnell. On the highway, there was a bad wreck on the side
of the road which seems to be holding up traffic. "Oh my God,
really? I am trying to get someplace, people." She was starting to get
very impatient and went around on the median to get to the exit she
needed to get off on to see Darnell. Dialing Darnell and waiting to
get to him, "Hey, where are you, Darnell? I just pulled up to the
Monaco Theatre Plex." He walked over to her car without her
knowledge and opened the door. "Boy! You scared me. Why did
you do that?" They both burst into laughter, and he hugged her and
said, "I got you, didn't I? Ummm, what is that fragrance?" He
squeezed her while still sniffing on her. "It's something by Estee
Lauder. I can't remember the name of it though. They come out
with something just about every month and you know I have to get
it." She answered trying to break away from the hug; let's go inside
and see this movie. "What are we going to watch? There are a few
good movies out this weekend you know, some action, intense
drama, what will it be?" He really didn't care as long as he could see

her. He wasn't up to any good. "Let's watch 'Playing for keep,' I hear it's supposed to be really hot. There is this dark chocolate fine brother in this movie and..." she would have kept going, but he cut her off. "Girl stop playing with me." They went inside and started on the movie. He put his arms around her and kept glancing over at her during the movie. She glanced back a couple of times and smiled at him. It was just like high school all over again; puppy love. Oh, how stupid she is for thinking this is okay; to be alone with an old flame and leave a good man at home. What part of this is good? What part of this is safe? The movie continued for about an hour and a half while they continued playing the game of peek a boo and flirting with each other. He kissed her a few times on the cheek to let her know that he got love for her, I guess. They had no idea of what was going on outside. It had started to rain really hard. Neither of them thought about looking at the forecast before going to the movie. It started to thunder outside, but inside of a movie theatre, you will always hear lots of noise with the surround sound and 15 movies playing at the same time. After the movie had ended, they walked back to the front while holding hands. Denise forgot that she was a married woman and has completely lost her mind. Does she not know that she's in public? This crazy chick. "Ring-ring," Chauncey was calling her phone, but she did not pick up right away. He called a second time, and she picked up, "Hey baby, where are you? Are you safe?" She answered, "Yes, I am going to stay with a friend tonight," Her phone hung up due to low reception in the area due to the storm. Back to Darnell, it was. They walked to the exit, and the rain was so heavy that you could barely see anything besides the lights. Darnell saw the Westin Hotel though. The siren on their cell phone went off for a thunderstorm warning, a lightning warning, and a flood warning. "Let's just run across the way to the lobby of that hotel, we can dry off, get something to eat and drink, and if we need to get a room, we will already be over there to do so." This dude ain't no good. "Okay, let's go." She wasn't thinking clearly. With all the noise around her, people chattering about the storm, the phones still going off, and Darnell in her ear, it was enough to drive her into a ditch.

They ran over to the Westin like they had planned. Her hair was soaked and looking a hot mess, he was looking sexy while dripping wet, and it threw her off even more. "I'm going to go ahead and get a room so that you can blow dry your hair," Darnell said thoughtfully; impressing her little naïve self. Chauncey started calling her phone but couldn't get through to her. He left about four voice messages so far and even sent texts to see if she was okay. "Come on, let's go upstairs and get in this room so that you can get dry; wouldn't want you getting sick." Darnell was so concerned and looked out for her, so she thought. They stepped on the elevator, and he continued looking at her in her eyes. "You look so amazing to me." He started speaking the words of flattery to her ears. "Bing!"

The elevator stopped, and they made their exit from the elevator and walked to their room to make the big entrance. He picked her up at the door as if he was taking her over the threshold. What a gentleman? He really should stop. "Let's take a shower together so that I could wash your hair like old times." He was very persistent in making her remember the past and the fun they had together. "I guess so, but you better not touch on anything but my hair." Poor thing, she really wants to flirt with danger. Why put yourself in a compromising position when you know that you could fall and hurt yourself or someone else? "I left my clothes in the car and..." she was cut off by the one with all the answers. "It's all good; I have seen all of you anyway. You shouldn't be ashamed to be around me in the nude. Girl come on." So, she did, she went into the shower. He first called room service to bring up a couple of items, and then he joined her. They laughed, talked, hugged and kissed. Once they finished in the shower, they walked slowly to the bed, but there was a knock on the door. It was just room service. Darnell walked over to the door with just his towel wrapped around his lower parts and his chest glistening with water still. "Hello, you ordered warm chocolate and strawberries?" The woman at the door was staring at him and looking at him up and down. "Yes, that would be for me," Darnell said as he received the cart and handed over a tip. He looked at Denise and allowed his towel to drop to the floor around his ankles. He was exposed and very erect. He was ready to make 'love,' and she was too.

They did the forbidden things, and he ate of the forbidden fruit. They did all of that, played around until late in the midnight hours. He fell asleep, but she couldn't even make herself shut her eyes. The guilty conscience will do that to you. There is no way that you can go out and hurt someone else by fulfilling your own selfish desires and still have peace afterwards when you have a heart. She wasn't thinking clearly; there was too much pressure and noise from Darnell to give her time to examine the situation. What if she had time to think? She would have known that thunderstorms won't last all night and that they could have stayed at the lobby of the movie theatre. She would have been able to see through Darnell and realize that it wasn't him, but it was something else inside of him controlling him; something called lust. She rose up from the bed and went into her purse to find her phone. She had forgotten about her entire husband back at home and a husband who loves and cares for her with his innermost being. But her crazy behind is up in the bed with another man; get out of here. Her phone only had seven percent battery left, and she tried checking his messages and voicemails, but her phone was not cooperating with her. I wonder how Chauncey is feeling right now.

Denise went into the restroom and put on her clothes quickly and got out of there. She got on the elevator, started to pace around and started to let the guilt get the best of her. The elevator stopped, and a little old couple got on the elevator. "Hello there, little lady. How are you? Were you held up by the rain last night too? My husband, Agnus and I went ahead and decided to stay here at the hotel. He's such a sweet man. Ever since I have known him, he's been a gentleman and has showered me with love. After fifty-two years, we are still acting as if we are teenagers." The little old lady glanced at Denise's ring, and asked, "Where is your husband?" Denise wasn't ready for that question and couldn't think of an answer fast enough. The elevator stopped, and she ran out as quickly as she could. She rumbled around in her purse to find the keys to the car and finally got inside. Her hands were shaking, her hair was a mess. She looked in the mirror and looked like this....

What a shame. Denise was running around looking a hot mess and having to return to her husband with another man's touch on her body, another man's kiss on her neck and all over her body and did not even take a shower before going home. She would have back at the hotel, but she knew that Darnell would wake up and join her for another round of love.

When she entered the house, Chauncey was on the sofa asleep. She felt guilty for making him stay up all night worrying about her grown tail. Instead of waking him, she ran up the steps and took a quick shower, cleaned her face, and put cream on her puffy eyes. Denise started to contemplate in her mind whether to tell her husband what she has done, how she betrayed him, how she stepped out on her marriage. The tears continued to flow from her eyes, and she started to gasp for air. She was mad at herself, disappointed in her decisions, and resentful towards Darnell. She started to regret that she had even rekindled an old flame and allowed the fires to spark the way that they did. Chauncey heard some noise, but he knew that she wasn't home, so he hurried upstairs to see where the noise was coming from. Grabbing at the handle of the bathroom door, he couldn't get inside because she locked the door behind her. So, he knocked. "Baby, what are you doing in there? When did you get home?" Nervous and frantic, she knocked over things in the bathroom trying to figure out what to say or do. She wasn't a cheater, she was just Denise, the girl who got caught up in a jam. "Hold on baby, I am coming out." She replied to him. When she finally walked out, she couldn't look at him in his eyes. She looked at his chest, down at the floor, and walked over to the bed. "What's wrong Denise? What happened? Is there something you need to tell me?" He asked question after question, and her reply was, "I had too much to drink." He knew that she was lying. Denise never drinks more than one alcoholic beverage, not even when she is at home. He knows that her beliefs on drinking were merely drinking red wine for the heart, not over indulging in it, and most of all, staying sober. He knew that she had done something wrong but did not even question her about it. He went downstairs after placing a blanket over her. He sat down on the sofa and let out a few tears, but he asked God to help him through it and help him be the man that he should be for her. "If I am not doing everything I need to do to keep her, Lord show me what to do."

Denise began to be depressed and didn't want to do anything but sit around the house. Sleeping through the days and having morning sickness; Denise did not know what was going on. She thought she might have come down with a cold or the flu, but when she missed her period, she grew very scared. There were a few pregnancy tests upstairs from the times she thought she and Chauncey were ready for a baby, but it never happened for them. All three of the tests came out to be positive. "God, why? This can't be happening right now." She had to tell Chauncey what happened but did not know how to tell him. He came upstairs to see what she was doing. "Chauncey, I have to tell you something." Chauncey put his finger over her lips and picked her up off of the floor and walked her over to the bed. "Denise, I already know, and I already forgive you. I love you, unconditionally." He held her while she cried. She couldn't believe that this man would stay with her after the dirt that she has done. "Why are you staying with me?" He did not answer her; he just continued to let her cry on his shoulder. He did not ever understand why she stepped out on him, but he still loved her and wouldn't let that end their marriage. He took care of her and also made sure she had everything she needed during the pregnancy. But after two months, she started bleeding and having pain in her lower abdomen. She had lost the baby and started to be depressed all over again. But Chauncey was there for her and with her through it all. He never brought up the Darnell situation, and never ridiculed her for cheating. He never thought that sin had caused her to lose the baby. He cherished her and made sure that he obeyed what he was taught. The woman was the weaker vessel, and he was to be the strength that she needed in their marriage. Instead of judging her, he started to build her up with confidence and hope, he spoke positive words and spoke life over her. A change started to happen. She started to believe again. She now knew that her mistake was forgiven and that he would never hold it over her head. She finally learned that she had to forgive herself and to stop walking around with the guilt of her sin. Their marriage grew stronger, and they were inseparable ever after.

Every person is not as forgiving as Chauncey. Chauncey could have gone out and cheated and had his fun with another female too. But what would that prove? He knew that it would be childish to repay evil for evil just because he was hurt. Chauncey wasn't selfish at all. Why go out and jeopardize your vows that you made before God and your loved one? Most people think the grass is greener on the other side. They think that they see something inside of the new grass rather than sifting through the grass that they already have to find new treasure. The grass is always green from a distance, it's attractive, and it is very smooth, cut really nice, shaped up just the way we like. But once you get all the way up on it, it is brown, dead, and withered. Once you really look at it and see that it is covered with the fakeness just to draw you in, you can stop yourself from stepping in that direction. To those that allow themselves to be deceived by it, there will always be counterfeit grass out there waiting on you. But if you already have someone that you truly love you; just communicate with them what kind of garden you would like to have and build their confidence so that you can both put in work together getting all the weeds out, without the third-party interfering with something that God created in the first place.

Chapter 3

Trust Me

Which way do I go, Lord? I don't know what to do, where to go, what decision to make, or how to get to where I need to be. I am tired of going around in circles, doing the same things, and settling down for anything and anyone. I don't know how to pick the right person to be in a relationship with. I do not know how to do much of anything without you. Where are you? I feel so far away from you at times. I know that you hear me. I just don't understand why you are not moving for me or answering me when I need you to. Maybe you have answered, and I just do not understand your ways. Maybe I am just ungrateful of what you have done and cannot see that you have my best interest at heart. Please forgive me Lord for being so selfish. Show me what to do, where to go, how to talk, and how to walk worthy. Please be that lamp to my feet and light unto my path like you said you would. I feel so lost right now. It feels like I am fighting to get somewhere, but I have no clue about the destination. All I know is that I want to be closer to you.

God- All you have to do is trust in Me.

Me- But how do I trust you? I try my best to give everything over to you, but it seems like I am carrying this heavy load on my own. My flesh wants to retaliate against evil people and every adversary. Problems come, and it seems like I am fighting alone. Why can't I feel you? How do I trust you when I can't see you?

God- Just trust me, my child. I will never leave you nor forsake you.

Me- Why do I feel so far away from you? Why am I not getting closer to you as fast as I would like to? I just want to feel different on the inside. I want to be restored and delivered from myself. Help me, God.

God- I am nearer to you than you think I am. Trust me; I will be with you until the end. I am your redeemer.

Me- Why do I carry around so much guilt and shame from the past? Why can't I let it go?

God- Trust me, my child, I have forgiven you and have thrown all your sins into the sea of forgetfulness. Learn to love and forgive yourself.

Me- Why do you love me even after all the wrong I've done? I've betrayed you, turned my back on you, hung you on the cross, and have done all manner of evil against you. But you still love me? What kind of God are you?

God- I'll never stop loving you. Even until the end of time. My love will never stop. I love you unconditionally. No matter what you have done my child, you cannot push my love for you away. I am the Omnipresent, omnipotent, omniscient God. I am the God that was, and is, and is to come; the same yesterday, today and forever more.

Me-   Father, I haven't been pleasing unto you, especially with my body. I've used my body for evil and not good. Aren't you mad at me?

God-   I am not mad at you. Just continue to humble yourself, seek my face, and turn from your wicked ways. I hear you; I know your thoughts from afar. I can read the contents of your heart. I know that you want me, and desire to be closer to me. I am here, standing by.

Me-   Why do you love me the way you love me, God? How can I love myself the way you love when I cannot see myself the way you see me?

God-   Trust me, perfect love takes time. You are getting there. You have to keep trusting me, keep believing, and keep your eyes on me. I will keep you, I will direct you, and I will teach you the right way to go. I will restore you, cover you, revive you, and keep you in all your ways. I will hear you before you call me and answer you before your mouth speaks a word. I will protect you and keep you safe from harm seen and unseen. My arms will forever be open unto you waiting to comfort you. You are mine, and I am yours. I see you, I hear you, and I am here for you. I will never let go of you.

Chapter 4

Inhale

So many times, we hold on to things and keep them hidden in our minds, never releasing it or letting it go. Tormented by our past, afraid to move ahead, we stay in bondage. Afraid of judgment from our peers, we act like everything is okay. Our life at home is a wreck, but out in public we smile and give hugs hiding our true emotions on the inside. Why can't we release it? Too busy worrying about what people may think, or how they are going to react, questions circulate in your mind. How will they look at me? Are they going to laugh at me? Am I going to lose my friends? What will they think of me? We forget about God. God is right there with us, waiting to hear our confessions and willing to forgive us for everything we have done. Everything, anything, even if it happened five seconds ago. He said that He would remember it no more. All He asks is that we repent and turn from our wicked ways. Are we ready to go to God? Are we too afraid of Him? Now is the time to come to Him. He said come while he is near, and he is closer to you than you can ever imagine. Come on, talk to God. It does not matter how much you have done, he will never get tired of listening to you, nor will he take his love away from you because of your sins. Inhale, and let it go.

"Dr. Ryan, your client has arrived," said the secretary as she walked Shannon Gates inside the office. "How are you doing today Shannon?"

asked Dr. Ryan. "I am fine," answered Shannon. "Is there anything, in particular, today you want to talk about?" asked Dr. Ryan. "Well, I do have a lot of things on my mind. I really feel like I am going to burst if I do not tell someone. My heart feels so heavily weighed down. I am so ashamed of my past that I cannot seem to get to my future. I have been carrying around guilt, pain, and unforgiveness on my conscience for many years. I don't know how to let it go," explained Shannon. "Well tell me, what does it involve? Where does the pain come from? Asked Dr. Ryan." "I think it comes from past relationships. I always thought I had to have a boyfriend around to hear a voice, or just to feel a touch. I put up with a lot just because I wanted to be with that person, just because I was lonely and wanted company." After all of that, I was left empty, sad, broken hearted, used up and felt worthless. The feeling that comes over me when I think back is that I am undeserving of a good man. I always felt like the situations happened because of me not being pretty enough, or not being sexy enough. Settling for just a guy with some of the things that I would like in a man, and finally seeing him for what he is and what he wants to receive from me has taken a toll on me mentally. How do I get back to the beginning? How does God look at me? Can God fix me? Does he hear me when I pray? I have been so far out there; will God still use a person like me? Will he still love me? I have done the worst things imaginable, and I do not know where to start to get my life fixed or my problems solved. How do I turn my life around? It seems like the more I strive to get myself out of this pit, the deeper I fall into it. The higher I get, the harder I fall. "I....need....help." Shannon breathes slowly in while tears flow from her eyes. Her eyes are red, puffy, and desperate. All she wants is change. She knows the right place to go and who to speak with but does not know how to ask. To an outsider, it seems easy to just ask for what you want. But when you are inside of the situation, the tables turn, and you're trying to figure it out just like Shannon.

"Shannon, you do not have to worry. God is aware of your pain; he is well acquainted with your grief. He knows everything you think of, He knows your thoughts from afar off. There is nothing too big for him to handle, too hard or heavy for him to carry, or too high for him to reach. He told us to cast our cares upon him, and that he cares for us. What we cannot do, God is able to do it. He said that all we have to do is ask him, right?" "Yes ma'am," answered Shannon. "Look, I want you to know that you are not alone in this world. There are a lot of women before you that have been through similar situations, some may have been through something a little more extreme than yours. A lot of people go through things to become a stronger person. God will not put more on you than you can bear. He gives us a way of escape when we are dealing with temptation, but it is up to us to use that door. He helps us when we least expect him to. Because of your honesty and your confessions, God will work a miracle in your life. He has read the contents of your heart and knows that you are sincere about wanting to change. He says, repent, turn from your evil ways, and I will hear from heaven, forgive your sins, and heal you. He wants to take care of you. He will never leave you. I want you to repeat after me, okay?" "Yes ma'am," answered Shannon. "Dear Father God, I am calling to you. I am asking you for guidance, strength, protection, and fulfillment in you. I know that I can only be complete in you. I need you in my life more than I have ever needed you before. I cannot make it without you, nor can I live without you. Every time I decide on my own, I mess up. Please make haste to help me, Father. Come and see about your daughter. I belong to you, and I need you right away. In the Name of Jesus Christ, I pray, Amen."

"How do you feel?" asked Dr. Ryan. "I feel a lot better, still feel a little empty on the inside, but I know that God will come in and fill me. I know that I have to have faith and that faith without works is dead. I know that he hears my prayers. It's just so hard sometimes not seeing things you want to see come to pass when you want them to. You ever go through that?" Dr. Ryan looked at Shannon and answered, "God's ways are not our ways, and his thoughts are not our thoughts. His ways are higher than ours. That's why it is important to be patient for Him. Let Him move and direct your life in His timing and in his way. We rush things and get in his way and wonder what happened to our blessing. If you sit back, let go, and let God, and breathe, you won't have to wonder or worry any longer. So today, you may feel a little better because I have talked with you and gave you some encouraging words; but I would like for you to start studying the word of God and really meditate on the scriptures that pertain to how you feel and what you are going through. You will see how God will change that sad and lonely feeling on the inside into joy and peace. He gives peace in the midst of trials, tribulations, storms, and every bad thing you can possibly think of. He will deliver you and bring you up out of this. Do not worry Shannon. God loves you. I have another client coming in about ten minutes, is there anything else you would like to discuss with me until then?" No, ma'am. If I think of anything, I will call and make an appointment for another session. Thank you so much for your time, I really appreciate it," says Shannon. "You are so welcome sweetie, and have a blessed day," replies Dr. Ryan. Shannon walked out of the office with her head lifted higher, and a lot of weight lifted off of her shoulders. She was eager to get in her word and ready for a change in her life. She realized that great change would come if she would just hold on to God's unchanging hand, and at that moment, she was able to breathe.

Dr. Ryan knew that she only had a few minutes until her next session, so she quickly swallowed a few sips of her mocha Frappuccino, ate a few peanuts and went to brush her teeth so that her client would not be disturbed by her breath. She said a short prayer to the Lord. She said,

"Father, please give me the right words to say to encourage the women and men that I talk to. Let everything I say be edifying to their ears and their hearts. I know that if it was not for you, I would not be doing any of this, but it is through you that I live and move and have my being. My wisdom and knowledge come from you God. I thank you right now in Jesus Name, Amen." As soon as she finished, there was a knock at the door. It was the secretary bringing in the next client. "Dr. Ryan, Asia Whitley is here to see you," said the secretary. "Thank you, bring her right on in," answered Dr. Ryan.

"Hello, how are you doing," asked Dr. Ryan. Asia looked up at her and smiled. Her smile was covering how she really felt on the inside. Her eyes watered up, and she said, "I am fine." Dr. Ryan grabbed a few of the tissues from the box and handed over to Asia. "Thank you," whispered Asia. "What's on your mind Asia," asked Dr. Ryan. Taking a deep breath in, Asia looked up at the ceiling, and then glanced at Dr. Ryan. "I have a problem. I feel so unhappy all the time. I don't know what it is that comes over me. I sometimes feel that no matter what I do, it is never good enough. My weight is up and down constantly. I can't get a boyfriend worth my time, seems like everything that I want is out of my reach," says Asia. "What is it that you want," asked Dr. Ryan. "Well, I want to have a figure eight body like Kim Kardashian. I want my body to match my face. Everyone says I have a beautiful face for a big girl, and that's all I get. I want to be a singer, but how am I going to be in front of the crowd, moving around, with them laughing at my body? I want to marry a good guy, but how can I do that when no one wants to approach me for the way my body looks? I do not know what to do." "Well, for one thing, you are very beautiful. But you have to want to be beautiful for yourself and not for others to accept you. You have to believe that you are beautiful. You cannot worry about how others view you, Asia. God made you beautiful. You were fearfully and wonderfully made. If you put your focus on God, he would be able to change what you cannot change. He can do the impossible in your life. Most people have their priorities mixed up. Instead of them wanting to please God, they want to please themselves," says Dr. Ryan. "But it is easier for you to say all that you are saying because you have a banging body. You look like a model, you are so beautiful. So how do you know what God can do if you have never been as big as I am?" Asia spoke too soon. Dr. Ryan got up and went to her desk, pulled out a photo album, and handed it to Asia. "Go ahead, open it up," says Dr. Ryan. Asia flipped it open and turned from picture to picture. She could not believe her eyes. Dr. Ryan used to be overweight also. "I am sorry for what I said. How did you...?" Asia was shocked, she could not finish her question. Dr. Ryan said to her, "I asked God to help me to learn to love myself and to keep my focus on him no matter how big or how small I would become. I also started fasting and praying. I stayed away from the television; the internet, magazines, and anything that would make me feel insecure about my body. I did not want to be like the women on the screen, but I wanted to be at a healthy weight. At first, it seemed like no matter what I did, I was stuck the way those pictures framed me as. But the more I stayed in my word, the more I fell deeper in love with God, and myself. I no longer went by what others said about me, or how they judged me. Instead of needing approval from people, I waited on God. He accepted me, told me how much he loves me, how he would never leave me. He said that he would give me beauty for ashes, and that is exactly what he did. I am a living witness of what God can do, and what his love is. He can transform you too. But you have to be willing to let go of some things in your life. Stop worrying about being accepted by people when God has already accepted you. Stop waiting for validation from people when God has already done everything in his power to make you beautiful. He said that you are His and that no one will be able to take you out of His hand. Here is what I want you to do, take some time out to pray and commune with God on a daily basis. Try to stop watching television for a week and turn off everything around you so that you can hear the Lord when he is speaking to you. Turn off the telephone for a few hours and just breathe. God will begin changing situations in your life if you take some time out for Him. You will begin to feel His presence around you. Once you get deeper in your word, he will get closer and grow deeper in you. If you delight yourself in him, he will give you the desires of your heart. Try to keep your focus on God and present your body to him as a living sacrifice holy and acceptable unto him and watch him perform miracles in your life. Take your mind off of the carnal and get in touch with the spiritual. Make God the center of your life, and I guarantee you, you will not regret it." Asia looked at Dr. Ryan as if she was in awe of her. She was shocked at the before pictures and the after pictures of Dr. Ryan that she decided to take in everything that Dr. Ryan had spoken and put it to work in her life. She was ready for a transformation today if possible, but she knew that she needed to get to know God first. "Thank you so much for talking to me and giving me some hope," said Asia. "You are so welcome. Just remember, God can do the impossible," responded Dr. Ryan. They both stood up and said a prayer together, getting in agreement with the Holy Spirit. It was time for Asia to leave. "I will see you again soon, hopefully with a different attitude than the one that I came in with." Asia smiled and walked out of Dr. Ryan' office. It was break time. Dr. Ryan needed a break really bad. She started to walk out of the office and head for the lobby until in front of her sat a young lady, bruised up and crying. Instead of taking her break, she decided to deal with the matter at hand. "Are you Simone," she asked. Simone looked up at her and put her hands over her eyes, still crying. "Why don't we go to my office?" They walked into the office slowly, and both inhaled. Dr. Ryan grabbed the tissue box and went into her mini fridge to grab a bottle of water. It was quiet for a moment. Simone had to regain composure before she could speak. Dr. Ryan asked her softly, "are you ready to speak?" Simone took a deep breath in and slowly exhaled. Her voice when she spoke was very raspy. She began to tear up, but she let everything out on the table regardless of the overflow of tears. She said, "I am in love with someone who I want to love me back. All I want is for him to do me right. I try so hard to please him and to make sure that he does not have anything to stress about when he is around me." Dr. Ryan asks, "Where are all the bruises coming from Simone?" "Whenever someone else is looking at me, says hello to me, treats me like I want to be treated, he beats me. When he is angry about anything that goes on at the job or in his family; he beats on me. I don't know what to do to make him happy. I let him know all the time that he is the only man for me, and I would never do him wrong. But he is still unhappy with me. My family tells me that I should just leave him, but I do not know how to walk away. It's hard to walk away from someone that you care about. Have you ever felt that way about someone? I mean, have you ever had so much love on the inside of you for a person, but they wouldn't receive it?" Simone asked questions waiting on a response from Dr. Ryan. Dr. Ryan stood up, walked over to her desk and took out some photos of women who were in toxic relationships. Some of the women she knew and some she didn't. She saved those pictures so that when women come in her office with similar situations going on in their lives, she can enlighten them on what could happen if they stay in that kind of situation.

Dr. Ryan said to her, "This was my friend Cheryl (She showed her a photograph of a beautiful young woman). She had been in an abusive relationship for eight months before she was killed. She thought that she was in love, and also thought that she could make her maniac boyfriend love her back. She thought she could change him by being sweet and forgiving. She cooked and kept the house clean, stayed at home to make sure she did not get accused of anything. Her boyfriend would get drunk hanging with the fellas and then come home to her, whipping on her and throwing her down the stairs. She still stayed around, hoping and praying that he would change. She felt like since prayer changed things, she should wait on God. I'm going to tell you like I told her, if someone is not willing to change, you cannot expect God to just do some 'abracadabra' on a person to make them change. God is a God of miracles and not magic. But even if he wanted to work a miracle to turn a situation around, the person has to agree. Everyone told her to get out and save herself. She had a lot of warnings before she was killed. In her heart, she felt that all he needed was someone to love him. She loved hard and showered him with gifts, and she hugged him even after he blackened her eyes and bruised her up. In the end, he beat her to death one night coming home after being drunk. I remember the last time that I saw her; she told me she had a plan. She had the biggest smile on her face while she told me. She said she was going to get pregnant by him and then he would change. In her mind, he was going to stop beating on her because she would be with child. Sad to say, she never got pregnant. Even worse, she died that same night. What do you think will happen to you if you stick around with your man beating on you? Do you think your love is actually going to stop his fist from going upside your head? Do you think that he will roll over tonight and just be that man that you want in your life? Nothing is going to change if he does not want it to change Simone. I want you to get this and get it good. Love is gentle, kind, will not hurt you, and it will not kill you. Your man will not love you the way you want him to because he does not know how to love. He was never taught how to love, and right now is not willing to learn. If you are willing to stick around for more beatings, then go right ahead. But your best bet would be to go back home to your mom until you can make enough money to get out on your own. Even before you get out on your own, you have to learn how to be strong, tough, and get some backbone. As women, sometimes we portray ourselves as strong women but are really cowards. Sometimes we are foolish and naïve. That's when men take over and do what they want to us, and we just sit back and let them. All the low self-esteem and insecure thoughts going through our mind is just the devil trying to attack us. The enemy wants us to think that we are not good enough for a man of valor, so we settle for the sorry guy that we think we can change into what we want. We try to mold a boy into a man. But I can tell you this, if you wait on God like I did, he will send you the right one in due time. Ask God to keep you until that time comes. Ask him to sustain you, protect you, establish you, and guide you. He will prepare you to be the woman you need to be so that when the right one comes, you will be what that man needs as a mate. But, if you decide to stay where you are, I advise you to go get a life insurance policy and make sure that you put the beneficiary as your mother. There is no need for everyone to go broke trying to bury anybody who makes a choice to die, right?" Simone looked up at her, and she was very shocked that those words would come out of her mouth. Who would actually talk about dying while someone is hurting is what Simone was thinking? But she knew Dr. Ryan was correct, and it was time to decide. It was either going to be life or death. Dr. Ryan made it very clear for Simone and painted the perfect picture so that she can see it for herself. It was about time for Simone to leave. "Thank you so much for being real and not sugar-coating anything Dr. Ryan." Simone smiled at Dr. Ryan, gave her a big hug and walked out of the office. Dr. Ryan had a feeling of peace come over her, and she released a sigh of relief. Some way, somehow, she knew that Simone would make the right choice. She thanked God for delivering Simone right away because you should shout before the battle is over. Dr. Ryan decided that it was high time for a lunch break. She went to the lobby, there was no one sitting there, so she decided to run to her car quickly before she is stopped once again. Her secretary called her cell and said to her, "China has called and rescheduled her appointment. She will come tomorrow instead. Your next and last appointment of the day will be at 3p.m."

"Thank you, Lord," Dr. Ryan said aloud. "I praise your name. There is none like you. Thank you for doing exceeding abundantly above all I asked you. Thank you for reading my thoughts from afar off. You are so amazing, God." She called her husband to see if he was free for lunch. He was indeed and met her at the restaurant. She praised God all the way to the restaurant. She had so much joy in her spirit. She and her hubby flirted like little teenagers. Tickled each other, said silly jokes, and enjoyed each other's company. It was a blessing to her to have a man who treated her with respect, who sincerely cared for her with getting something in return. Dr. Ryan was blessed and highly favored. Mr. Ryan asked her, "Do you have time to see a movie?" "I sure do," she answered. "I have a couple of hours to spend with you." They both smiled at each other while eating their food, and then Dr. Ryan raised her hand in the air for the waiter to bring the check. She was not the type of woman who always waited for the man to pay for everything. But she was lucky to get one that did not like her paying for anything. He felt uncomfortable when she paid for things. He wanted her to have everything and wanted to give her everything. In her past relationships, men always took from her. She was a sincere giver from the heart, and guys took advantage of that. But now she has a man, a real man. She does not have to worry about being used up, treated wrong, or being left alone. This guy took his vows serious, and he is really in love with her. The waiter came over to the table and handed her the check, but Mr. Ryan took it out of her hands and said, "Girl, stop playing." He took out his card, gave it to the waiter, and then smiled at his wife. She smiled back and stood up so that they can head out. He helped her with her jacket and gave her a big kiss on the cheek. He said to her, "I love me some Mrs. Ryan." She said, "Boy, you know I love you too." They went to the movie theatre and watched the new James Bond movie. They enjoyed themselves, and she had to head back to work. "I will see you later baby," she said to him. "I will see you for dinner. I am going to try out this new recipe I saw on Emeril live show yesterday. I can't wait to see you tonight girl." They both smiled and kissed each other goodbye and went their separate ways.

She got back to the office and could not stop praising God for a real man. She knew it could be nobody but God because every single time she would get with someone that she thought was the right one, he would let her down. This man that she has now, he's just awesome. "Dr. Ryan, your client is here." The secretary was standing at the door and waiting for the client to come through the door so that she can shut it. "How are you today?" Dr. Ryan asked, still smiling about the date she just had. "I am fine," answered Mercedes. "So, what is on your mind?" I can't get my boyfriend to stop cheating. I do not get it. I love him so much and treat him right, but he still goes out and sleeps with other women. He says he loves me, but why can't he stay faithful? He always buys me things, spoils me all the time, and says I do not have to work. He wants me to relax, and to stay pretty. What is wrong with me that he can't just be with me? What is the problem here? What am I missing? Am I too skinny? Do I need to gain some weight? Do I need butt pads or something? Maybe I should get some implants, and he may start looking at me a little more than he does. I am so confused right now. I just don't know what to do. While Mercedes started tearing up, Dr. Ryan got the tissue box out and allowed her to use as much as she needed. Dr. Ryan waited for her to stop talking and crying before she began speaking. It was obvious that Mercedes had become insecure due to her man cheating, but also that she is afraid of leaving because she would miss out on getting spoiled by him, getting everything, she wanted, but nothing she needed. After Mercedes finally calmed down, she slowly took in a deep breath and scooted all the way back on the sofa as she exhaled.

Dr. Ryan stood up and took her vest off. She walked over and opened the closet door to put it on a hanger. She took her time with everything she did. Dr. Ryan did not want to rush. It seemed like she wanted to give Mercedes some time to think about everything she just said. Only a simple person would think the way Mercedes was thinking. She walked over to the mini fridge and pulled out a green tea for herself; and a cranberry Snapple for Mercedes. They both took a sip of their drinks and put the lid back on. Dr. Ryan said to her, "Now Mercedes, do you think a man is going to love you if you alter your appearance? Do you honestly think that there is anything you can do to yourself to make anyone love you more? If he cannot love you right now, what makes you think he will love you later? Some people have a sickness, and some are just plain stupid. They do not know what they got until it is gone. Both men and women alike do things outside of their relationships trying to fill voids or trying to portray what they have seen growing up. A lot of people call them generational curses, but I think it is up to the individual to make a choice. We have choices. We know when something is right and when it is wrong. But if you choose not to be delivered, you will stay that same way. If you continue trying to change yourself, Mercedes, just so this man can be faithful to you, then you will continue to waste your time being unhappy. He's not looking at these women because they have big boobs or big butts. He is sick in his mind. He wants to have it his way all the time with whomever he desires to have it with. He is not worried about her body, or your body. He is feeding his appetite. Why are you sticking around?" Mercedes looked down in embarrassment. She couldn't find an answer. Dr. Ryan asked her, "What are you good at? Do you have any aspirations, any plans for your life? Or do you suspect he will just stay with you forever while he is doing his dirt and still take care of you? Do you think he is going to marry you? What kind of woman are you portraying by staying while he does his business with some other woman and comes home to you and kiss you? When he finally does have sex with you, how can you be certain that you will not catch anything? You do not know if he is wearing condoms with the other women. You don't know what is going on because you are not there. He can tell you anything, and you have no choice but to believe because you want to stick around with him and wait for him to change. What you need to do is get a life." Mercedes looked up at her with a confused look on her face. Dr. Ryan continued. "A life of your own is what I mean. Do something with yourself. Get a job, your own place, and live. You do not have to allow a man to do you wrong just because he is paying the bills and buying you whatever you want. You can be happy by yourself. Trust me, I did it for years. Right now, you are not even happy. You are stuck between a rock and a hard place. You want to wait around for this man to love you. How can he when he does not know what love is? He has not been taught. He has not seen love growing up, and that is why he feels the need to have sex with whomever and wherever. Sex is love to him. That's all he knows. Why don't you leave him, continue to get counseling so that you can get in a better place? You need to grow spiritually and get stronger mentally. It all takes time, but it can be accomplished. Once you realize that God is able to bless you with someone who can really love you, take care of you, and cherish you, the better off you will be. You want to be with someone who will be faithful, sincere, honest, trustworthy, and loves God most of all. Why not just allow God to help you grow, prepare you to be who you need to be and allow him to bring to you who you need in your life? He is more than able." Mercedes said to her, "I don't know if I am good enough for a church guy. I just want someone to love me." Dr. Ryan said to her, "You deserve to be treated with respect. Right now, you are just going through that insecure phase due to your man running around on you. I've been there and done that. It is going to take some time for all those ill feelings and doubt to dissolve. Once you get to the place where God wants you to be, you will feel a lot better. You will look back at the situation that you are in and wonder, "What was I thinking?" Just give God a chance. You been in enough relationships, gave enough people a chance, allow God one chance. He will change your life forever." Mercedes took another deep breath in, and said, "Since you know best, I will give God a try. I have never taken this route before, but he must be awesome since you keep saying his name." Dr. Ryan laughed out loud, and said, "He is more than awesome. He is an amazing God. He can do the impossible in your life only if you allow him to. What seems too hard for you is never too hard for God. You will find out though. Just stay faithful to him; he will bring you so much joy." It was the last session of the day. They both stood up and got their jackets on. Dr. Ryan walked Mercedes to the lobby and told her to "Trust God." Mercedes smiled and walked out of the building. Dr. Ryan went back into her office to make sure everything was in order for tomorrow before she left out. She made sure she shut down her computer, and then she looked at her schedule for tomorrow. She had only two clients tomorrow. She was excited to get out of the office.

Remembering her husband telling her that he would cook, she ran to the car and put her music on. She praised God all the way to the house. The song that she kept on repeat was "I am an overcomer, by William McDowell." She knows that she is an overcomer by her testimony. Arriving at the house, she didn't see any lights on. She did see her husband's car though. "Maybe he fell asleep," she thought aloud. When she finally got inside, there were candles lit in the dining room. He was waiting for her in the kitchen. He took off her jacket and hung it up, took off her heels, and slowly walked her in the dining room where he had flowers all around the table and all over the floor. He pulled out her chair, and she sat down. Her smile was so big. She couldn't wait to see what he cooked. He took the cover off of her food, and it was grilled salmon with a homemade dipping sauce, steamed vegetables, rice, and croissant rolls with melted butter and honey. They said grace and thanked God for providing food for them. She said, "Thank you, Jesus, for my wonderful husband." He looked at her and smiled. They ate their dinner together and talked about the movie that they went to see earlier after lunch. Once they finished eating, he said to her, "Follow the rose petals upstairs and relax while I clean the dishes and put everything away." She did just what he asked her to. Once she got to the end of the rose petals, she ended up in the bathroom. Around the tub, there were rose petals and candles. Her favorite book and a glass of apple juice were sitting there also. She smiled and looked up to heaven and said, "Thank you, Jesus." She got in and started reading her book, she relaxed, and all the things that were talked about today in her office were no longer on her mind. She sat her book down after reading a couple of chapters, laid her head back and closed her eyes. She couldn't seem to stop smiling. Once she finished, she realized that her towel was on the heater so that she can stay warm while drying off. She put on her pajamas and went into the bedroom to see where her hubby was, but he was still downstairs. Once she got back in the kitchen, she saw there on the countertop, a plate with a slice of cheesecake with strawberry topping and sauce on it. There were two forks on the plate, but she didn't know where her hubby was. He walked in the kitchen, grabbed the plate, and her hand, and led her into the den where they enjoy their movies together. He put on one of her favorite movies. Dorothy Dandridge as Carmen Jones played while they sat there and ate their cheesecake together. She fell asleep a little while afterwards, and he turned everything off. He carried her upstairs and put her in the bed and covered her with the covers to make sure she would stay warm. She slept through the night without being awaken by outside noises like dogs, cats, or rowdy neighbors fighting over nothing. She slept peacefully with her hubby by her side to hold her and protect her if she needed. In the morning, the birds chirped, and the sun shined through the window on her face; she began to smile. She turned over and saw that her husband was still sleeping. She raced down the stairs to cook breakfast for him. She sang 'I'm so into you' by Tamia while cooking her hubby's food. Just to be married to a great man who actually loved her and took pride in taking care of her, it made her the happiest woman on the planet. She walked up the stairs with a plate of scrambled eggs, cheese grits, four slices of bacon, and croissants covered in butter and honey. On a separate salsa, she had sliced strawberries, kiwi, and blackberries with a big tall glass of pineapple orange juice which was his favorite. She sat the tray down beside the bed on top of his night stand. To wake him up, she gave him kisses all over his face. She knew that he hated when she kissed him all over the face, it would wake him up fast. Once he opened his eyes, she shouted "good morning baby! I made you breakfast, I hope you like it." Placing the tray on the bed so that he can enjoy his breakfast, she walked away quickly to get ready for work. He must have been really hungry, once she got out of the shower, his plate was spotless, and he was already fast asleep. Instead of waking him back up, she just took the tray downstairs, cleaned the dishes and headed to work. Giving thanks, she worshipped and praised God the whole way to work. Dr. Ryan knew that it was God who got her to the place that she is right now, not her degree, not her husband, and not her family. She worked hard and stayed in faith, and God blessed her. She remembered that faith without works is dead. That's what she intends to teach her clients, without prayer, you will not receive anything. You have to ask to receive something from the Lord. She pulled up to work and had joy in her heart and a big smile on her face. Walking inside the lobby, her secretary was there waiting for her with hot green tea and two spoons of honey. "Good morning Dr. Ryan, how are you?" "I am great Gabriella, how are you?" Dr. Ryan replied. Gabriella smiled and followed Dr. Ryan in her office and placed her green tea on the desk, helped her with her jacket, and also updated her on the appointments she will have today. "You have a 9:30am with a China Silverman, an 11:30am with Kylie Buccannon, and your last appointment is at 2:30pm with Solomon Taylor. You are also scheduled to meet up with your sisters in between your 11:30 and 2:30 when you get a break. Don't forget. Have a great session." "Thank you," replied

Dr. Ryan as she pulled out her bible. Reading the Word before sessions and praying for direction for the right words to say to her clients from God was her everyday routine. She always felt peace and joy afterwards, so why not do what is pleasing to God if you are going to feel great afterwards?

China arrived as soon as the secretary got to her desk. "Good morning, I have an appointment with Dr. Ryan." "Sign in right here and have a seat. May I offer you some water?" Gabriella asked. "No thank you," replied China. Dr. Ryan came out to greet China and to escort her in the office. She was not like other doctors. She always came out to greet, and to establish a strong, trustworthy bond between herself and her patients. She wanted them to feel and see that she is not high-minded, or too good to come out to the lobby and talk with them. She remembered everyday where she came from, so she made sure to stay humble wherever the Lord took her and to be faithful to everything He blessed her with. "What is on your mind? Is everything alright?" Dr. Ryan was very concerned with her clients and wanted to make sure that she was led by God with the right answers to any problems they may have. "I feel so heavy on the inside. My heart sometimes feels like it can no longer take any of the weight that is already on it. I grew up in the church. I know what's right and what is wrong. But I got caught up into something that it seems extremely hard to get out of. I want to do what is right, but something keeps pulling me and tugging at me. The grip that this thing has on me is so tight. I know the devil is after me and has been for a long time. I am trying to get out of this. I need to get out right now. I want to please God, but it seems like no matter what I do, I let Him down. I know he is not happy with me. I am going against what I have been taught; I have fallen short of his word. I know that the bible says the wages of sin is death, but how do I get out of sin?" China was so humble, she was trying to get everything out without actually saying what it is that she is doing wrong. Dr. Ryan looked at her and smiled before she could actually say anything, she looked at China with admiration. China is nineteen and just started college, but she already knows that she needs to be delivered instead of waiting until things got really messy for her. "It is very hard to stay focused with people in your ear telling you to come on let's hang out. They probably have parties and fine guys and everything that is tempting to the flesh available for you everywhere you turn. That is the devil's job. He is always on his job to persuade, and deceive, and to seduce you. The devil comes up against those who know what is right so that they can fall. He comes for a season and leaves and comes back stronger than before. He knows you desire to do what is right and that you want to achieve something with your life. He does not want you to be anything. He's destined for hell, and he wants you to be a part of his crew. There is nothing too hard for God, China. God can reach to the lowest of the low, and to the farthest, and the highest. There is no one greater than God. He is our salvation, our helper, our healer, our protection, and our deliverer. Whatever you need from God, all you have to do is ask. He is a just God, willing to provide for you a way of escape. He will bless the just and the unjust, why would you be exempt?" China looked up at Dr. Ryan and looked back down. She started fiddling her fingers around and looked as if she wanted to say something but was too embarrassed. "What is it China?" Dr. Ryan asked as she continued to watch China sit there with her head down. "Well, can God deliver a lesbian? I am actually bisexual, but I tend to mostly have a relationship with females. I am attracted to men, but I am afraid to be hurt again. I don't know what to do. "To you China, it may look impossible. But with God, all things are possible, if we believe. You have to put your trust in God. Not in man, not in a woman, but God. His word says; my grace is sufficient for thee: for my strength is made perfect in weakness (II Cor. 12:9). When we are weak, our God is strong. That's what you have to remember China. God's love is stronger, bigger, deeper, and wider than anything you could ever imagine anything else is. Stop worrying, God hears your every prayer. He knows what you need. He said to cast your cares upon Him, He will give you rest (Matt. 11:28-30). I want you to start believing that God is able to deliver you, set you free and that he will never leave you no matter what, okay China." China was half smiling and somewhat of a doubtful mind. She

70

knows that she has to start reading the bible on her own. If she continues to live off of what others say, how will she ever know for herself how it feels to have a relationship with God? "Well, I hope by the next time I see you, you are smiling, and you have something amazing to talk to me about." Dr. Ryan smiled as she innocently patted China on the side of her arm. "Yes, ma'am. I hope so too. I will be reading and studying for myself. Thanks so much for taking the time out to talk to me, China said softly. "No problem sweetie. Everything is going to be alright. I will see you next time." Dr. Ryan walked her out to the lobby, and they said goodbye to each other. Dr. Ryan looked around and did not see any of her clients just yet, so she rushed back in her office and got down on her knees to pray. She prayed for China. She knew the importance of interceding for others, especially those who do not know how to pray for themselves. She skipped her usual snack and green tea, and she took a thirty-minute communion with God. It is more important to eat up the word sometimes, especially when you need God to move. Dr. Ryan was no stranger to fasting or turning her plate down. She wanted to do this while it was on her mind and still strong in the air, instead of waiting until she got home.

There was a knock at the door. It was Gabriella notifying her that her next client is in the lobby. Dr. Ryan got up and put her bible away. She went to her private washroom to wash her face and freshen up. Going towards the door, she looked out the window and saw the sun shining and glistening through the trees. "Thank you, God, for a beautiful day," she said to herself before walking out to the lobby. "Hello Kylie, how are you?" She waved her hand to direct Kylie into her office. She could have stayed out in the lobby for Kylie's session. Kylie never stays over twenty minutes. Kylie is really shy and has a humble and quiet spirit. She is very sweet and soft spoken. "I am doing great," answered Kylie. "I just wanted to take up a few minutes of your time. The last time I was here, we talked about my biological mother that I have never met. I did locate her, and she was very happy to see me. It hurt me a lot to see someone who gave up on me when I was just a baby. I wanted answers. I was confused, and I did not want to like her at all, but my heart would not let me hate her. Her story was, she was on drugs really bad and did not know what else to do with me besides put me up for adoption. She tried to find me after she became sober, but because of my new parents changing my name, she could not find me. I am happy that I did get to see one part of where I came from. My dad died two years after I was born. I met his mother. She was happy to see me especially since I am her only grandchild. We sat down and talked for a little while about how daddy died. She said someone shot him. He was just at the gas station pumping gas, two guys got into a fight, and one took out a gun. They did not try to shoot him, but the gun went off while they were wrestling with the gun and shot him. The guys were very remorseful because a lot of people knew my dad and knew that he was a great guy. Everyone loved my dad. My grandmother said a lot of people showed up at his funeral. She told me all kinds of stories about my dad and how he wanted to keep me, but my mom wouldn't let him. He was educated, and a hard worker. She showed me pictures of him. I look just like he did." Tears rolled down Kylie's face as she continued to talk. "I wish I could have met him. He wanted to keep me, to take care of me, and to be there for me. But she wouldn't let him. Why would she do that? Why would she keep him away from his daughter? Now he is gone." Dr. Ryan reached over to hand Kylie some Kleenex and to console her by rubbing her back while she cried. Dr. Ryan said to her, "Everything happens for a reason. We will not always know the answer. But we must remember to accept what God allows. What if you were with your daddy when he got killed? You wouldn't be here today. Some things come to make us stronger. We don't always understand God's plan, but we have to trust that he knows what is best for us. His ways will never be our ways, and our thoughts are different than his." Kylie thought to herself, and then said aloud; "If everything is on His terms, then what am I here for?" Dr. Ryan looked at her and smiled. "God has a perfect plan for you, a ministry within you to help other young ladies." Kylie stood up, smiled and said, "thank you for talking with me today, I have to run." Dr. Ryan walked with her out of the office and told her to "trust God." Kylie smiled and said, "I will see you later." Dr. Ryan walked back into the office, sipped some of her water, and took a deep breath before talking to God. After spending time with God, she remembered that she was supposed to meet up with her sisters. She changed her clothing while dialing one of her sister's numbers. LaToya picked up the phone, "hello." "Hey LaToya, what are you doing? What restaurant are we meeting up at?" Dr. Ryan was asking too many questions at once. LaToya said quickly, "hold on, I have a call coming in." She clicked over, and it was her other sister, Shirley. Shirley was on her way to the spot where they were supposed to meet up. "Where are you at LaToya, are you on your way?" Latoya replied, "Yeah, to Olive Garden, right?" Shirley said, "Yes, get on the road now." LaToya rushed off of the phone, "okay, okay, I'm on my way." LaToya clicked back over, "Jackie, we are meeting at Olive Garden right now so head that way." "Okay," said Dr. Ryan, "I am on my way."

Dr. Ryan headed out of the office and said to Gabriella, "I will be back in a couple of hours. Take your break and be back at 2pm. Call me if you need me, bye." Once she got in the car, she turned on 90.1 FM radio station, and her song was on. It was CeCe Winans singing Alright. Dr. Ryan sang right along with her, "Alright, alright, alright, keeping your head up high no matter..." She drove to the restaurant with praise on her lips. She was so excited to see her sisters. When she got inside, they all hugged each other and smiled like they have never seen each other before. They all chatted a bit until the waiter came to take their drink orders. "Hello, my name is Walter, and I am going to be your server today. Have you had enough time to figure out what you want to drink?" All of the ladies looked quickly over the menu, and Shirley said, "I would like some White wine and a glass of water." LaToya said, "I will just have some Red wine, and a glass of water also." Dr. Ryan said, "I will just have some strawberry lemonade, and I am also ready to order food if my sisters are." "We are not ready, and the only reason you know what you want is that you always order the same thing," Shirley said and continued to talk. "You need to try something different this time." Their server decided to give them some time to look over the menu while he fetched their drinks. "No, I am going to stick with what I know, Dr. Ryan said. "Okay LaToya, have you decided on what colors you wanted for the wedding?" "Well, I thought of just cream and violet or cream and purple color. I love purple you know. But I was thinking, instead of me wearing a white or off-white dress, I decided to wear purple, and I want the rest of the wedding party to wear the cream. You all might be wearing ivory, off white, cream, or something of that nature." "Wow," said Shirley. "I have never thought of anything like that before, neither has anyone else pulled that off. It sounds unique, and whatever you want to do, we will do it." LaToya looked over at Dr. Ryan and said, "Jackie, what do you think?" Dr. Ryan said to her, "I will wear whatever you want me to wear; it's your day baby sis." The waiter came back with their drinks. "Are you ladies ready to order food? "Yes," said Dr. Ryan. "I would like the shrimp scampi, with a house salad." Shirley ordered spaghetti and meatballs, and LaToya had salad and soup. Both of the older sisters looked at her; wondering why she only ordered salad and soup. "What's going on, is everything alright sis?" Dr. Ryan asked her sister while waiting for a reply. "Yes, I just want to make sure I can fit into my wedding gown. I have already put on five pounds after the fitting due to stress. Right now, the best thing for me to do is watch what I am eating. I want to be able to fit my dress and have room to breathe without trying to suck everything in." LaToya went on and on like she usually does. "So, do you have the seating chart, and the guest list all figured out?" Shirley asked questions about the wedding while Jackie was daydreaming and absent from the conversation. They all ate, drank, and were merry. Soon it was time for Jackie to head back to the office for one last client. She said good bye to her sisters, and they all agreed to meet up again next week. "I love you both; I will pay on the way out. You both enjoy yourselves. I will see you later." Dr. Ryan placed money on the table for the tip and headed to the front to pay the tab. She walked to her car and was anxious to hear what was playing on the radio. It was John P. Kee. "A throwback huh?" Dr. Ryan started singing along. "I never shall forget what you've done for me." She praised God all the way back to the office, and she was filled with so much joy in her heart. Dr. Ryan walked inside, and her client was already there waiting. "You are a little early; I will be right with you." She hurried in her office, put her things away, and said a prayer to God. "Come on in Sir. How are you doing today? Your name is Solomon, right?" "Yes." He answered without a smile. "Are you okay? You look as if something is hurting you." Dr. Ryan wanted him to open up and start talking, but he couldn't right away. There was a lot of anger inside of him. He was hurting, his heart was broken, and he didn't know what to do. He knows that he cannot fix himself. Only God can help him, mend his broken heart, and make him whole again. Dr. Ryan sat there with him and consoled and comforted him as much as she knew how. She allowed him to cry, she allowed him to lie on her shoulder. After about ten minutes, he started to release what was on the inside. "My heart is so heavy. I have been trying for years to look past what has happened to me, but I cannot stop thinking about it. I know that I have unforgiveness and anger in my heart. I cannot forgive what was done to me. I don't know how to. Why should I forgive people for molesting me? I did not ask for it. Why should I forgive someone for taking my innocence away? Why would God allow me to go through that type of pain?" Solomon started to cry again. He has a lot more to say, but just thinking of it brings the sorrow and grief to his heart. He is in so much pain from the past. "You have to stop harboring unforgiveness in your heart. Forgiveness is what has your future, and your past will continue to stand right here before you, until you learn to forgive. If you cannot forgive anyone for things done to you, how do you expect God to forgive you of your sins?" Dr. Ryan spoke softly and ever so gently. It was almost like a whisper; she wanted to keep Solomon calm and his mind at peace. But that did not work. Solomon's eyes widened and were filled with rage; while he yelled in anger. "You expect me to forgive my uncle for raping me? Is that what God wants from me? So, he wants me to forgive people who raped me and molested me and forced me to do all manner of immoral things to their bodies? One of my uncles raped me, my older cousin used to fondle with my penis, and my babysitter made me suck on his genitals, and then he also raped me. So, you are telling me to forgive these people!" Solomon started to scream, he stood up and walked to one of the empty corners of the office and kneeled down. He could barely breathe. He continued to talk, "I do not understand God. Why would he allow such an evil thing to happen to an innocent child? I do not understand why I have to forgive them when they are the ones who should come to me and correct their wrongs. Why am I the one hurting so bad? Why can't I move forward? And why did God allow them to move on with their life?" He started gasping for air while tears rolled down his face. "Here you go, drink some water." Dr. Ryan brought over a bottle of water. She wiped the tears from his eyes, and slowly helped him off of the floor. They walked to the sofa together, and she hugged him. She knew that this was not something that would be changed overnight, but she knew that she had to help him as much as God allowed her to. His body trembled as she held him. She rubbed his back, and she started singing a song to help calm him down. "I feel far away, but I can hear you calling me; bound in chains, but yet you say I can be free. I feel wounded, but yet you say I can be whole; I get weary, I know there's rest for my soul. I feel so afraid you can take away my fear; lonely. Still, your presence lingers near. Sometimes I am insecure, but I find confidence in you; when I am overwhelmed, you know just what to do. Then you say, you understand, exactly where I am. With your love, your perfect love, you draw me once again. So, I come boldly, to your thrown of grace, to obtain mercy, in my time of need." She continued to sing softly as it quieted his soul and brought peace to his heart. After she was finished, he said to her, "Oh that I had wings like a dove! For then would I fly away and be at rest." She realized that those words were from the book of Psalms and that he knew some of the Bible. She smiled, and God spoke a word to her. God told her to invite him to her bible class and to the prayer meetings that they have. "I would like for you to come to my church for bible class if possible. You do not have to join, I just want for you to attend for a couple of nights." He replied, "I might come one night, right now, I am not too sure. I haven't been to church for ten years. I did not give up on God; I just gave up on him helping me. It seems like the more and more I try to forget my past, it is ever present before me. Why won't God take that away? Why won't he just allow me to forget everything that has happened to me? I would like to forget it all, and to start anew." Dr. Ryan said to him, "But how will you be able to help with the healing of others who have been in that same situation? How will you help them have hope and faith in God? You are going to be used by God to minister to those hurting like you are, some worse than you. Allow God to heal you. Let God fix everything in your life that is broken, Solomon." "How can I help people when I can barely help myself?" Solomon asked her in curiosity. "If you stop trying to help yourself and allow God to help you, everything will turn out the way it should be. But if you continue to fix yourself, and keep the anger on the inside, you will probably stay the same or things might get a little uglier than they are." They talked for about fifteen more minutes. He was already over his time, but she didn't mind. She loves helping people, and she has given herself to God so that he can use her. However, God wants to use her, she said it is alright with her. They stood up from her sofa, put on their coats, and prepared to leave out. He was the last client of the day, so she decided to do something a little differently today. She walked him to his car and as they walked slowly; she gave him words of encouragement. She said to him, "Wait on the Lord: be of good courage, and he shall strengthen your heart: wait, I say, on the Lord (Psalm 27:14). The Lord is my rock, and my fortress, and my deliverer; my God, my strength, in whom I will trust; He is my high tower. In thy presence is fullness of joy; at thy right hand, there are pleasures for evermore (Psalm 16:11). It is God that avenges me and subdues the people under me (Psalm 18:47). I will bless the Lord at all times: his praise shall continually be in my mouth. My soul shall make her boast in the Lord (Psalm 34:1-2). Solomon smiled; he started to feel peace in the midst of his storm. He knows that it will take some time for him to forgive and learn how to let everything go. He is willing to take the steps necessary to stay in the race and get back in the place where he needed to be so that God can use him. Before he got in his truck, he asked her, "What cd was that song on that you were singing?" She answered, "Malinda Watts. I have it in the car; you can have it if you like. I know all the songs on the cd, and have it saved to my computer in the office and at home." He looked at her and asked, "Are you sure?" She said, "Yes, it's yours now." He said, "Thank you, and gave her a hug." He got in his car and put the cd in. Today was the beginning of restoration for him.

Dr. Ryan got in her car and started talking to God and thanking him. She said, "Thank you God for wisdom, thank you for peace that surpasses all understanding. I thank you, Lord, for mercy and grace. I thank you, Lord, for renewing of the mind. I thank you for being so awesome in my life. I thank you for my life, health, and strength. I thank you for being my provider. I thank you for being a rock in the weary land. I thank, and I praise you for loving me, God. I give all the glory and honor to you

God. It is you that made me and created me, and I am not my own, but I belong to you Father." She praised and thanked God all the way home. Her job would be stressful for someone who did not have God in their life. But having God strengthening her and giving her peace of mind every single day helps her. She does not have to go talk to a counselor or psychiatrist. She talks to God. The ultimate counselor, the keeper of her soul, her helper in the time of trouble; God is who she talks to and depend on. She arrived home, when she looked down at her phone, she had three missed calls. "Who could be calling me?" It was her hubby. He was worried about her since she was running a little later than usual. "That man loves me, thank you, Jesus, for my husband." He came outside and over to her side of the car. He opened the door, and said to her, "Baby, please don't do that to me again." He smiled at her, and she smiled at him. They walked slowly while holding hands, and he said, "Lord I thank you for my beautiful, virtuous, sweet wife." She smiled at him and said, "Baby, you are making me shy." They walked in the house and talked about how good God was over dinner that was prepared by Mr. Ryan. She was at awe; God gave her everything she needed. God blessed her with a man that cooked dinner and wasn't waiting on her to come home to do everything. God knows what we have need of, even before we ask. Man, ain't God good.

(To be continued...)

Chapter 5

You

While staring in the mirror at my flesh, my soul, and my spirit, the reflection relentlessly gazed back at me. Her eyes spoke words to me while her lips were in a stern stance. She said some things that activated my tear ducts to release the biggest tears I've ever cried. Although I knew already, all of the things she said were true and needful to hear, it pierced my heart. She continued speaking, while I drowned myself in regret and shame, I continued to listen and began to cover my face. She sternly said to me,

"you didn't love you enough; while out searching for what you thought you unreadily needed, you should have been spending time alone; getting to know your 'self.' You didn't think before moving or acting. You continued to do things you said you wouldn't do and then you turned around and blamed others for the situations that you couldn't seem to get yourself out of. You! You did this to yourself. You got yourself to this place of unrest, anxiety, and insecurities because you did not want to listen to the instructions given to you from women who've experienced these same encounters before you even set foot on earth. You couldn't hear them over your loud head voice telling you 'this is a new day and age.' You didn't honor God while opening your legs up to men who do not and will not ever care for you, love you, or cherish you. For if they'd have any care in the world about you, why are they 'so gone' now? Where have they disappeared to so quickly? Why have they deserted you like waste and have already run on to their next victim? They left you here with me."

I cried the heaviest cry while sitting here getting told off by the girl in the mirror. She wasn't completely finished going in on me...

"You forgot about God, and you left him behind while you got your groove on. You cried uncontrollably like a little girl letting her Father down after every encounter of sin because of conviction, but you still could not stop. You did not have the power to stop. Well, at least that is what you thought. You've been told that Your Father will never leave you nor forsake you, but you could no longer feel his presence near you, and you could not hear his voice. There were several occasions where you called to him, but you didn't get the response you were expecting. You told Him, if he gets you out of this, you will never go back. You told Him you will wait for Him to bless you. But hardheadedly and rebelliously, you went back time and time again to please this, this flesh that had been crying out for a touch and longing for security. You had become engulfed in the lust of the eye and the lust of the flesh and had taken on the pride of life. You didn't know the flesh was evil, it just looked so darn good to you. Why yes, it's a beauty to look upon, and yes, it feels good to be caressed and held by someone else. By the time all of that is over, you are back at the very beginning. You are still lonely, you are still lost, you are still empty, you are still broken, you can't move forward, you feel stuck, you are confused because you thought he loved you and you loved him. After the brief encounters, you feel as though you're easily manipulated, you are all over the place, and this is just all because you didn't know You."

There were days I thought to myself, am I just imagining these words from this mirror. I am looking at myself and hearing things that I'd rather not hear right now, especially while I feel down. I know that I am not perfect, but I also know that I can do better; I just don't know what to ask, where to start, or who to turn to. Is there really an issue though?

"You didn't know how to respect yourself, but yet you asked others to respect you. You knew I desired to be respected, but you continued choosing the ones that could not see things your way. You could plainly see that they wouldn't respect you, but you continued on striving with them believing that they would eventually change by you showing love towards them. But their words were convincing and the total opposite of their actions. You allowed words to sink into your ears as sweet lullaby's, and you stepped in the traps that were sat before you and schemes that were too transparent for you to miss. You lost your footing, the snare was gripping you so tightly, but at the same time when things felt so good, you started to forget the promises you made to your Father. Your No's were turning into Yes's, and instead of pushing away, you held on for the ride of your life. You were caught up by words. Words, promises, lies, intellectual bull crap, and deceitful captions that would have gotten these guys a 4.0 on the GPA in the class for guy fooling girl while her eyes are completely open. Just for a few seconds of pleasure. Pleasure? What is it? Is it all about sex? For you? Could you think of anything else that would bring pleasure to you without going against your Father's Will? There are so many things you could be doing, for instance, helping others, reading a fascinating book, volunteering somewhere, or even helping someone else so that they won't have to spend too much time in the mirror of their soul trying to figure it out like you are right now. You wanted to do things on your own, in your own timing. You should instead try to stay busy doing something productive that will produce good fruit. Stop giving in to words of deceit before you miss out on what is really for you. Real people will pass you by if they know that you don't care about the real You. You cannot ask God to bless you with anything if you aren't willing to let go of your fleshly desires, thoughts, and sinful actions. You cannot ask your Father to trust You if you aren't willing to trust yourself."

I tried to regroup by bending over the sink to splash cold water on my face and patting it dry. I wiped away the tears, took a few deep breaths in and out to calm myself of my own disgust and wondered if God still sees me. Does He still care?

"It's time to get a closer relationship with God so that He can show you, You. Perhaps if you are sincere in your desire for a closer walk with Him, you will hear the instructions He's been giving you all this time. But you have to be real in your thirst and hunger after that which is right. It's going to be tough at first because there are so many chains of bondage weighing you down, God will have to take all of that off first. You may still feel far away at first, but just know, God is right there shaping you and fixing you, and in the end, He will complete you. And because you are coming to Him with a repentant heart to seek a better way for your life, your joy, and your peace, He will recognize that as such, forgive your sins, and make you whole."

The girl in the mirror is you. She knows you better than anyone else. She knows when you are hiding something on the inside, covering up pain and scars, regretting some of your mistakes, and wishing for better days. She knows because she's been there too. It's time for you to start caring about You, Respecting You, Loving You, and most of all, allowing God to help You. He's able to resuscitate, rehabilitate, restore, revive, deliver, heal wounds, mend brokenness, repair damaged places, make you whiter than snow, give you a rebirth in Him, and remember those sins No more. It does not matter what you've done, it does not matter how many times you fell down, it does not matter how much you think you owe anyone, just give it all to God. He wants to help, so why don't you let Him Help You?

Chapter 6

Unequally Yoked

Being raised in the church does not mean that you are saved or delivered. Joshua found that out the hard way. Although he is saved and delivered, he's still a babe in Christ. He was out in the world once but did finally welcome God in his heart. He knows that Jesus died on the cross and rose on the third day. But when he started looking for a wife, he went about it the wrong way. He wanted her to be a beautiful woman in the church. How many of you know that when you ask God for something, you really need to be specific? Joshua thought that if she were in the church, she would be a real woman of God, and she would also know how to be a wife. Unfortunately, a lot of sinners go to church also; just to sit and look the part. I am not talking about people who mess up from time to time because of temptation. In this case, I am speaking of those who are willfully sinning every day and are asking forgiveness every day; knowing that they are planning to do the same thing all over again tomorrow. Whether it's cheating on the spouse or stealing, lying for no reason, or being deceitful, they are there. Yes, the bible says "all have sinned and have come short of the glory of God. But it also says, shall we continue in sin that grace may abound? God forbids." Beware; the wheat and the tares do grow together.

Joshua has an engineering job. He got his degree and saved up some money. He wanted to get everything in order because he knew that he desperately desired a mate. He bought a nice family sized home. His home has three bedrooms, two and a half baths, an extra room for an office, and a three-car side entry garage. God has shown him favor, and he is blessed because he has more than just the mustard seed of faith. He is faithful in giving, and he has the love of God in his heart. He is growing successfully both spiritually and in the natural. Joshua thought he was ready, and he went to search for a bride because it says, "A man that finds a wife, finds a good thing, and obtains the favor of the Lord." But you must wait on the Lord also. Listen to Him, wait on him; do not jump the gun. If you move too fast, you may end up with a Jezebel kind of lady. He was in a hurry because his flesh was craving something and needed to be fulfilled. And he read in the Bible, "It is better to marry than to burn." To burn with sexual desire that is. He did not want to get outside of the will of God. He decided it was the right time; he could not wait any longer. He saw Tiffany every Sunday at church, and she wore long dresses, and she seemed to fit the profile. She had on no make-up, no jewelry, and all of her dresses went past her knees. He saw the older faithful women of the church dress this way, and he wanted to make sure that when he is married, he is married to someone who in the future, would still be in the church. Tiffany was in the church, but the church was not in her. She was not in the Word, the Word did not abide in her, and she also did not have a personal relationship with God. She was doing what she knew to do because of being taught that way. Go to church on Sunday, wear a skirt, put stockings on underneath, and do not put on any make-up. Her mom taught her these things. But these things do not make you saved or delivered. Joshua sees that now.

How they met

Joshua saw Tiffany during church and said hello when she finally looked his way. She waved back at him and smiled. After church, he asked her will they ever be able to hang out if she could find the time. She said yes, and they did. The first date was awesome. They talked about what they wanted out of life and how they planned on getting it. After the date was over, she was anxious to get home to read her book. She just bought a new book that was detailed from beginning to end. It was like a romance novel, something that she enjoyed occasionally. She did not say to him what kind of book she was reading. She simply said, "I have to get home to do some reading." Joshua thought to himself, a woman who reads her Word, I like that. He did not know; it is not his fault. They would hang out from time to time. She had never been over to his home, and he had never been to hers.

After several months of dating, Tiffany started to wear make-up. Not that it was her first time, she just wears it periodically. It wasn't caked on her; Joshua did not notice it too much. But depending on how dark it was outside, the more she had on. She gave him some excuse to why she did it and asked him, "Do you mind me wearing makeup from time to time?" He said no because he did not have a problem wearing makeup, he was not aware of her wearing makeup. A few months go by, they are really feeling each other, and they decide it is time to get married. They did have questions in the back of their mind on whether or not it was too soon, but they still wanted to get married because they thought it was love. He thought he had found a woman who reads her word, but little did he know the rest of Tiffany's life was far worse than what was presented to him. Being patient is good. It is hard, but still good. Wait on God be of good courage.

They get married

They are now married and moved into her home. She wanted to stay at her place. He wanted to please his wife and make her happy, so that's where they moved to. He finally got all of his items into the home. Well, all of the items that she would allow him to bring in. He could not bring his sofa; it did not match her wall color. He had actually just got it from Ashley's furniture. He could not bring his sports memorabilia; she did not have a room for that, and it could not go into the living room. They had three bedrooms besides the master suite. But one of the rooms was used as her office space, another for her clothes because the master closet was filled up, and another room was for the guests. They just moved in together, and he thought that it would get better after a while. But it only got worse. He was still trying to be in the honeymoon phase, but there was a big lack of honey. He tried to stay calm about everything, but it seemed that he was being tested. He was not being tested. He should have waited a little longer before trying to marry someone he barely knew. Tiffany did not know how to cook. She knew how to keep the house clean and spotless though. I mean why not? She had O.C.D. He did not know this either. He did not notice that while they were out for dinner, she would clean their table before they ate and make sure their eating utensils were perfectly clean. He was blinded by beauty and the words of her saying she is going to read; that he was not paying any attention. Now knowing that she is a clean freak, he had to get on her routine of how things are run around her house. Yeah, it should be theirs, but it turns out just hers. He lives there though. There was a certain closet for her shoes and his shoes. He had the smallest closet, the smallest room to work in, and the smallest portion of the California king bed. She had an excuse for everything, and instead of speaking up, or causing confusion he decided to keep quiet and see what happens.

Darkness comes to light

Everything about Tiffany was not on the surface yet. She was having book club meetings with people. They would come over to the house and go over what they had read that month. When she would have a book meeting; he would shoot hoops or get someplace off to himself to read and study God's Word. But this particular day, he was at home and could hear everything that was going on. This book did not sound too good, he thought to himself. He stood outside of the door to really hear what was going on; and what was being said. He was very disappointed in his wife. He thought she was saved. He did not see this side of her before. He walked in on his wife reading one of the parts from the book. She was saying, "and then he put his penis inside my....," and he walked in to see what the heck was really going on. She told him to "get out! This book club is for women only." He told her, "We need to talk." She told him, "As soon as this club meeting is over with, I am all yours." The women laughed as he walked out of the room. He went outside to talk to the Lord. He was very angry. He did not know marriage would be this hard.

All of the women leaving out of the house had looks on their faces as if they knew what was about to happen. She was straightening up the area where everyone was at for the meeting. She went out to look for her husband so that they can talk about it. She was ready to argue. She had everything that she wanted to say in her mind already. Nobody was going to tell her what to do or how to do it in her own house. She asked, "Joshua, what the hell was that about in there? Do you think that that was appropriate? Coming in there interrupting me while I am in the middle of a meeting don't seem to be what Jesus would do. You thought that you could just bust the meeting up because you felt like it? This is my house, okay. You don't disrespect me in my house in front of people." He knew that if he said anything, it would add fuel to the fire. And the fire was already roaring and smoking, so he thought that it was best to walk away. A soft answer does turn away wrath. What did he get himself into?

When the sun came up, Joshua decided to start the day off fresh. He remembered the word of God where it says, His mercies are new every morning. He cooked breakfast, and he took it up to her while she was still in bed. She woke up, looked at him, and asked: "Do you think that you are forgiven?" He was very confused with his wife, and wondered in his mind, "If loving and kindness can draw a sinner to God, why can't I draw my wife?" He did not know what to do. She got out of bed, turned on her music, and went to her office space to work on a project that has been overdue for a while. She was jamming to Jeezy and later had on some Lil Wayne. He could not believe his ears. He did not even know that she knew this type of music.

Girl's night out...

It's Friday, and it is time for some much-needed fun. She wanted to let loose and forget about all the crazy mess that was going on at home. While she was getting dressed to go out at ten o'clock, he was reading his bible. He did not know what was going on upstairs. She had her music going loud and hard. She had put on her body suit and some red heels. She turned off the music and walked down the stairs still singing. "Tiffany, where are you going dressed like that?" he asked. She replied, "It's girl's night out tonight." "You are not leaving out of the house looking like that," he said. She turned around with a crazy look on her face ready to slap somebody. "What do I look like?" she asked. He said, "You look easy, you look like a whore with that get up on." She said, "Well you know what you look like, a weak nigga. You are always reading your bible, always praying to God. You never want to go to the club with me; you never want to listen to the music I listen to. You don't want to do anything I want to do." She stormed out and left him standing there in disbelief. He could not believe the words that came out of her mouth. He did not ever see this coming. Now he is really afraid to see what comes next. If it is not one thing, it is another.

She comes back to the house with the help of some of her friends. She is a little tipsy. She smells like smoke and cologne. He sees that she has been partying a little too hard. He stands there for a minute to look at his wife. He is hurting on the inside. But he remembered his vows that he spoke before God. For better or worse, through sickness and in health; is what he promised in front of the church and God during the wedding. Now he had to back it up. He does love his wife; he just hates the way she is. He picks her up, takes her up the stairs and gives her a shower. He put on her pajamas and laid her down in the bed. He said a prayer for her, and he left out of the room. He slept on the couch and had sweet dreams. He had been fasting and praying for a couple of days. When you marry the wrong person, you are going to have to pray more and fast twice as much. Trouble teaches you how to pray and fast. He has never prayed this much in his life. But it is drawing him closer to God. The more and more he prays for her, the worse she gets. He is still walking by faith and not by sight.

It is now morning; she comes downstairs and sees him on her sofa sleeping. She does not approve of that. Tiffany walks into the kitchen to fill a cup with water and throws it on him. He wakes up, and she acts a fool. "Was that necessary?" He asked her. "Well, how else am I going to get you off of my couch? Do you know how much I spent on this sofa? Huh? Do you think I want you lying all over my furniture? Why didn't you sleep in the bed?" She asked question after question. I guess that is why they said it is better for a man to be on the rooftop instead of in the house with a nagging wife. He gets up, without saying a word; takes a shower and leaves the house. She is very upset. It made her a little hot that he did not go back and forth with her. She wanted to argue, she wanted to make it seem like he was not a good husband. Yes, she realized that when she woke up, she had been showered, dressed, and placed in bed. But she did not want to say thank you, she did not want him to get the glory for being an awesome husband. She does not realize that he was doing what God would have done for us. God loves us, even when we are broken down, filthy, disgusting, and when we are evil. He comes in and cleanses us and makes us whiter than snow. She was not thinking at all. She had something else in mind after he left out of the house.

Tiffany goes upstairs and finds her address book. She calls one of her guy friends. She tells him everything that is going on; from her perspective. He does not give her any sound advice. Her friend Michael tells her, "If he can't make you happy, find someone who will." She is taking advice from someone who does not know God. She finds her purse and looks through her phone. The fine light-skinned guy at the club wanted to holla at her. She thought that it was time to make that happen. After all, Michael did say someone else can make her happy. How is she going to know unless she experiments? She calls the number. A woman picks up, "Hello?" Hi, I am calling for Brian, "Tiffany replies. "Hold on one moment baby." She calls out to Brian, "Brian, some girl is on this phone for you, don't be on my phone long." "Shut up with all that hollering dang," he said to his mom. Tiffany is laughing softly. Brian comes to the phone, "Hello?" "Yeah, this is Tiffany, the girl that you gave your number to last night at the club," she said, grinning from ear to ear. He replied, "You da one wit da big tits?" She replied, "No, the one with the long hair and pretty skin." He asked, "The one with the Mercedes?" "Yeah, that's me. So, what are you doing right now?" she asked. "Well I am chilling over at my mom's house," he replied. "Do you want to come over my house for a while, so that we can get to know each other?" He replied, "fa sho, fa sho. What's your address?" She gave him all the information, and she got ready. He was over there in about five minutes. Someone had to drop him off because he does not have a car. She did not realize that he lived with his mother, and he does not respect his mother and that he does not have a car. Red flags were popping up all over the place; she was blind. Poor baby couldn't see a flag even if she wanted to. He gets out of the car and walked to the door and started saying little things under his breath. "Yeah, Ima have to go ahead and move in here. This is nice right here. Looks like a little palace for a king like me." He did not know proper grammar or the proper anything for that matter. He banged on her door with one hand while holding his pants up with the other. Guess he already knew what time it was, so he really didn't need a belt. She came to the door with her robe on. He said, "What it is 'tho'?" She opened her robe and had on a see-through chemise and then they went at it.

All day at work, Tiffany has been on her husband's mind. He prayed and talked to God. Joshua decided to get off work a little earlier than usual. He wanted to get some flowers and a card for his wife. She did not deserve it. He had love in his heart. He wanted to make his marriage work. So, he pulled up to the house, and he got out quietly because he wanted to surprise her. So, he unlocks the door, but his wife is on the couch on top of some stranger. They are both naked, on the same couch that he was not supposed to sleep on.

He dropped the flowers, and the card, and stood there in disbelief. He was shocked, dumbfounded, and baffled by the whole situation. She jumps up, and while putting on her robe, she asks, "What are you doing home so early?"

Brian gets up, laughing because he knows that he just broke up this relationship. Joshua says, "How long has this been going on?" She asked him again, "What are you doing home so early?" Brian gets his clothes on and sits down on the sofa. Joshua asked him to leave. But it wasn't happening because Tiffany wanted him there. She told him "You can leave; you don't do anything for me anyway." "This is my house, my stuff, and you did not contribute to any of it," she yelled out. "So, you can just get all of your things, and get out. We are done," she finished. Joshua actually did just that, packed up his things, and got out of there. He did not have a lot to pack because most of his items were in storage. He stayed in a hotel for a week until he found a nice place to stay. He moved back into his home. He kept the house that he bought, and he was grateful to be smart enough to do so. He had planned to lease it or rent it out but decided to just keep it.

Tiffany is about to wake up

Brian moved in; from his mother's house into Tiffany's house. She was happy for a little while. He was doing all the things she loved to do. They listened to rap music together, they hung out with friends and talked about clubs, parties, drinking, and smoking together. She spent money on him and spoiled him with everything. She did not see any bad in him yet. She divorced Joshua and stopped working as hard. She even took weeks off at a time just so that they can go on vacations. She showed him her world. He did not show her anything but a good time in the bedroom. He did not give her massages, could not cook, could not clean, did not know how to speak good grammar, and did not put up with a lot of talking back. They were out, and he told her to buy him a watch that was about $300. "Heck no, that is too expensive." She talked back, and he did not like that. He said, "Well we are going to see about it." She was still talking, running her mouth like she usually would with Joshua, and he waited until they got in the car to put his hands on her. He hit her right in the mouth. That was when she found out who Brian really was. She had moved a man of God out, and Satan in.

Over the next few months, things began to get a little worse. She did not know what to do. She was cleaning up after this man, cooking for him, and catering to him. The only thing he did all day was sitting on the couch, watch television and drink beers and wine. He left the house sometimes while he went to go visit his kids. He had about eight of them. They range from two to five. He wasn't paying child support. The girls refused to put him on it. He treated them so good, still giving them good loving every now and then. Tiffany did not know where he was going every single day in her

Mercedes; she did not even dare ask any questions. She became a prisoner in her own home. The home that was supposed to be shared between her and Joshua has been overtaken by a strongman. She has been losing weight from stress, hair is shedding really badly, and that pretty skin she once had is now bruised up.

She was demoted on the job and then she was later fired. Her Mercedes was repossessed. Her boyfriend was selling dope, but not enough to pay bills. He beat on her for losing the job and left. After all, he was expecting her to take care of him. He had already used up more than half of the money. He moved back in with his mom, and now Tiffany was left alone. She was very unhealthy looking, but she had to go look for a job. She found a little part-time gig that could hold her over until she found something else. But she could not get to work on time due to the bus hours. So, she had to find rides. None of her friends had time to give her a ride, seems like she was out of luck. She had to quit that job and find something a little closer to home; a job within walking distance. Tiffany did get the job at the supermarket down the street. She made nine bucks an hour and was making ends meet; just barely.

Joshua came into the market one day. He was looking good. She had never seen him so fine. Not that he looked bad before, but now he does not belong to her. She can see so much clearer now. After all, her money was faded, and the beauty, it took all of that for her to realize that all he wanted to do was love her. She could not keep her eyes off of him. He did not even see her. He grabbed his cart and went shopping for groceries. He was putting so much food in the cart; you would think he was shopping for a family. As luck would have it, he got in the line where Tiffany was the cashier. He still did not recognize her. After putting all of his groceries on the belt, he looked at the screen. He just waited for the total. Tiffany said, "how are you today Joshua?" He said, "I am blessed, and you?" He thought for a moment, and then asked, "How do you know my name?" She replied, "It's me, Tiffany." He looked at her still trying to figure out who she was. "Tiffany who?" he said with a look of disbelief. In his mind, he is thinking, "this cannot be the same Tiffany I was married to just six months ago." But it was. She asked him, "Can I speak to you outside for one minute?" He said, "sure, no problem." He really felt sorry for her. This is the same woman who was exalting herself because of beauty and money, mistreating him and being unappreciative. Now her beauty has faded, and she has no money. His heart grew heavy for her. He went outside and waited on her. She came out there with a pitiful look on her face. She said, "Josh baby, give me one more chance. I realize that I made the biggest mistake of my life. I regret the way that I treated you, and if you give me a second chance, I promise I will do you right. I will be better. I will go to church and get saved for you, and I won't cheat." Joshua was not stupid enough to even take a chance on her again. Even though he felt sorry for her, and had some love for her, he could not do that to himself. She did not want to get saved for herself; she wanted to get saved for him. God had something better for him. He told her, "You really need to get healthy; you do not look so good. I will pray for you and pray that God sends you someone that qualifies to your standards. I hope that you have a great life. And Tiffany, I forgive you for all that you have done to me." At that very instant, he felt like everything that weighed heavy on him was lifted off. She asked him, "Can you at least help me?" He pulled out a wad of hundreds, and he gave her ten hundred dollars. It's so funny how God will make your enemies your footstool. He told her to be blessed and walked away with his groceries and loaded his Range Rover.

It was time for him to get to his girlfriend's house. The groceries he bought were for her and her two kids. They are soon to be his kids also. But he had planned to cook for them. He could cook really great. Almost as if he was a chef, he could throw down in the kitchen. He did not mind them coming in to help him a little. They enjoyed being in the kitchen together. He always imagined how his family would be, and now he sees it. He does not regret at all the things he went through with Tiffany. He is so much stronger, and he can survive hard times. He is patient, calm, and loving. He was everything a woman could want in a husband; a good woman that is. He finally found his helpmate, and they are setting a date to get married. If we wait on God, He will send that special someone to us. But that is only if we allow him to. It's time out for being in a hurry for lust, and actually putting time in for Love. God is love and love is of God.

Chapter 17

Come

An impossible situation to us is always possible with God. Believing is the first step to turning the negative impossibilities into positive possibilities. Michelle did not know that what she needed was possible with God. She stayed on this same ride for quite some time now. Afraid to get off, she just let doubt consume her. Well, that is until God came into her life. He offers us life, health, and prosperity. He wants us to have the best. Sometimes we throw our best away. All we need is help from God. That is exactly what He is about to give Michelle, some help.

Michelle always had a boyfriend. She couldn't live without one. When she did not have one, she felt miserable, did not know what to do with time. When she was alone, she felt like she would lose her mind. Men were her god. They were her master. She thought that if she had a man around, she would feel loved. But it was not so, they just used her up every time. She wanted to feel needed, but they took all her goods, they took her pearls. Those old swine were just playing with her mind and her heart; laughing at her. She was used to those rough guys, hard looking, hooligans and such. She never had a sweet and handsome guy as a boyfriend. On Friday night, it was club night. Everyone always gathered at her home to get dressed, stamp their faces with makeup, and dance around until it was time to go. She and her girls all liked the same type of man. What she really needed was Jesus.

Michelle was young, vibrant, and had a beautiful heart. She did not know what God had given her, she did not see herself the way He did. She felt unloved when there was no man around to hug her, to kiss her, to use her, to mistreat her. Michelle had a lot to learn. God placed something special down inside her, but it was up to her to understand and take hold of her gifts. She has to believe and receive it. He cannot make her act out on the gifts and talents that He placed inside of her. But He is right there every step of the way, waiting on her to ask Him for help. His arms are wide open, waiting on her to run to Him. After all, asking is the only way you are going to be able to receive anything. Michelle needed guidance from someone who has been through the same things she has. She needed someone to let her know that she does not have to have a man; she does not have to sleep around. She saw her mom do the same thing as a child. There was a generational curse over her life that has been there for years and years, it just needed to be broken. She was in desperate need of deliverance. She has been hearing something inside of her, telling her to run forward, and don't look back. But she does not know what that voice is, where it is coming from, and whether it is speaking to her for sure.

One evening, Michelle was at the grocery store just buying a few things. She was near the milk, and there was a 'little lady' over by the milk in the way. The lady said to her, "How are you doing sweetie?" Michelle said, "I am fine, and you?" The 'little lady' said, "Well, I am blessed and highly favored in God. I am still standing up by myself without a cane, I am holding on to God's unchanging hand." Then she added, "Are you holding on to His hand daughter?" Michelle looked at her, she did not respond right away. The 'little lady' said, "What church do you belong to?" Michelle looked down as if she was embarrassed for not going to church, she replied, "I do not go to church." The 'little lady' said to her, "Well you do now. On Sunday we have Sunday school at 9:30a.m., and worship service at 11:00a.m. We are located on 6th Avenue, right off of Triana Blvd. The name of the church is Hand of God Ministries. I cannot wait to see you there sweetie." Before Michelle could reject the invitation, the lady was gone. It was like she vanished, disappeared into thin air. Michelle looked down the aisle, she went past each aisle, and still could not find this 'little lady.' She went back to the milk aisle to grab her milk, she had forgotten all about it. Right after she grabbed it, she saw a card on the floor with the information on it for the church. The 'little lady' had dropped it some kind of way, and Michelle took it as a sign. When Michelle stood there thinking, she recalled that the little lady did not even grab any milk out of the fridge. It was like the 'little lady' was standing there waiting on Michelle. It was meant to be, things happen how they are meant to and when they are meant to. That 'little lady' was sent by God to Michelle, and it was up to Michelle to take heed to what God had asked.

After long thought, going back and forth in her mind, Michelle was just too nervous to attend any church. She thought that they would laugh at her. She thought that they would see right through her, all her sins, all the evil she has done. She did not want to go to church and be embarrassed. Little did she know that every sinner needs to find a church and sit on the front pew. But in her mind, she thought that she needed to work on herself first, and then go to church. The devil had her thinking that she was the worst person in the world. He had her feeling like God would not be pleased with her, due to her sexual immoralities. She did not know that God was the forgiver of all sins and that he redeemed her from the curse after hanging up on the cross. He died for all sin and offers abundant life to all that come unto him. But something in her ear said, Come. She looked around. She did not see anyone, she put the television on mute, and she sat still on the sofa. She did not hear anything, so she lay back down on the sofa. She took the television off of mute, and the voice came back to her again. Come. Michelle got nervous, she ran upstairs, closed her door, and she lay down in the bed with the covers over her head. She whispered to God for the first time in her life. She said, "Lord, I know that it has to be you talking to me, I am going to come." God does hear our faintest cry. She fell asleep right there in that spot and had sweet, peaceful sleep. She woke up the next morning, looking for something to wear to church. She looked all over the closet for a dress that would come to her ankles. She thought that that was the dress code for godly women. She did not know that clothes did not make a person more saved. It was her heart that actually got His attention. God did not look at her outer appearance, nor was he concerned with what she chose to wear. A voice came to her, "Come as you are." So, she went to take a shower and ironed her clothes. She wore some jeans and a nice blouse and some cute little sandals. She got her purse and keys and headed on out.

When she got outside, the car did not want to start at first. She sat there, and she thought to herself, I just had my car checked out. She tried to crank it up again, and it did start up. The devil started up early, yes, even on Sunday morning. She got down the street, and the car started shaking really badly. It was almost like it wanted to cut off. She sighed out loud and looked up as if she was going to pray to the Father. But before she could say anything, all the rumbling stopped. Before we pray, he answers, and while we are speaking, he hears us. What concerns us, concerns our Father. She got down near the church, but there was a train there on the tracks, not moving. She did not know what to think. Looking at her watch, she was already ten minutes late. She started getting the feeling of turning around and going back. At that very moment, the train moved out of the way. She got across the tracks and got to the church house. She went inside, and everyone was just sitting there. She thought to herself, "is it already over?" The congregation greeted her and welcomed her in like she was family. She took a seat; and all of a sudden, the 'little lady.' The 'little lady' that she had seen at the grocery store was up in the pulpit. She looked at Michelle and smiled. The little lady said, "God is going to do a work in here today. Harden not your heart and the Spirit of God is going to flow through this place today. Souls will be saved and delivered this day." She then introduced her husband as the speaker for today, and she sat down.

It was testimony service. People stood up and told what God had done for them this past week. One of the ladies said, "I did not know how I would pay my mortgage this month. I thought I would be evicted, and have to move back in with my mom, but God. God made a way out of no way. My mortgage is paid up for three months now. He blessed me in such a way that I cannot even explain. He opened up a window from heaven and poured me out a blessing that I did not even have enough room to receive it." Tears flowed from her eyes, and tears flowed from Michelle's eyes. Then a man stood up, he told of how he was in a car accident. He said, "There is no way that I could have escaped out of this car without a scratch on my body, no injuries at all. My car flipped over eight times, and I am standing here today without a scratch, without broken limbs, and with no damage to my brain. It's because of the grace of God. God is a good God, he is a saving God, He is a keeper, and He is a protector." Everyone praised God with him, they all thanked God for being an awesome God. After a few more testimonies, it was time for praise and worship. Sister Shantel Fuller and Sister Raven Meeks lead some songs, and the congregation joined in. The spirit indeed filled the place. It was a sweet aroma, an atmosphere that brought you tears of joy. You could feel the presence of God in the place sho-nuf. There was a heavy cloud filling the place, God's glory was being revealed.

That was the first time Michelle ever felt something so strong, but so good at the same time. She wept quietly to herself while she sat there in her seat. She knew that God was real, but she did not ever experience anything like this before. She did not pray, she did not read her Bible, she just knew that she was here on earth because of God. But she was going to find out more about him today. Pastor D.E. Barney got up and asked for Sister Jessica Williams to come up to sing a solo. She sang a song that was meant just for the right person to hear. Michelle needed to hear this song. Jessica did not know that she needed to hear it, but God did. He placed it on Jessica's heart to sing a song by Hezekiah Walker. Oh Lord, I have sinned, but you are still calling my name. When Jessica got to the part where she said, "How many times, do I go against your will? Then you forgive me, but yet I still, I turn around and do the things, the things I shouldn't do," Michelle burst into tears. She felt like that song was for her, and that she wanted change in her life. She did not want to do things that were wrong. She wanted to be taught. After the song was over, Pastor Barney got up and told everyone to bow their heads while he prayed. Before he started the sermon, he said, "God is a forgiving God. But you have to believe it for yourself. Ask him for forgiveness and see won't He do it." In the agreement, his wife, the little lady said, "You better say that." He asked everyone, "Open your bibles first to the book of Mark 5:36. We are talking about believing today. While believing God, we have to stand on His word and His promises. He said in Mark, be not afraid, only believe. All we have to do is believe. We have to believe in Him and His word. God is not a liar; His word will not lie. We should not be afraid to stand on the word of God. He did not give us the Spirit of fear. Even though we mess up from time to time, God still says the promise by faith of Jesus Christ will be given to us if we believe (Gal. 3:22). All we have to do is believe saints. If we come to God, we must believe that He is. Believe without a doubt in our heart, nothing wavering, and He will reward you." He preached about thirty more minutes, and it was altar call. He allowed Evangelist Brown to take over for alter call. She did pray over the people, and she laid hands. When she got to Michelle, she said, "God loves you, sweetie. No matter what you have done, God loves you. Don't let anyone tell you

112

any different. He asked you to come, and you came." Michelle was nervous, "How does this woman know that He told me to come," she wondered. The Evangelist said, "You stepped out on faith, you believed, and God is about to perform a miracle in your life. All you have to do is ask. He knows what you need, but He wants you to ask. While you are asking, keep believing that he has heard you, and it is done."

After altar call, it was offering time. Michelle was very nervous. She did not have a lot of money, and she thought it would be like it was on television. She thought they would ask for a $100 line and a $150 line. But that was not the case at this church. The Pastor said, "Get your offering in your hand, and let us stand to decree and declare our promises." Some of the things that they spoke were really interesting to Michelle. He said, "Repeat after me, I am the head and not the tail, I am above and not beneath, I shall be a lender and not a borrower." They made their petitions, and they gave their tithes and offerings. He prayed over the offering, and it was time for announcements.

Sister Shantel came up with her notebook and refreshed everyone on what Pastor preached about. She then gave the announcement to anyone who would like to come to the Women's Ministry taught by Sister LaReetha. "We have it every other Monday, and you are welcomed to come and be a part of this." She then proceeded to give the schedule of which their church services are held, "We have Sunday school at 9:30am, Sunday Worship at 11:00am, and Tuesday night prayer at 7pm, and

Thursday night Bible Study at 7pm. In your free time, you are welcome to come out and enjoy God with us." The little lady stood up and asked the visitors if they wanted to say anything. Michelle was too shy to say anything, so she just smiled and shook her head no. The little lady said, "Well, you are welcomed to come back and join us anytime. You are like family here at the Hand of God Ministries." Pastor Barney came back to the pulpit to dismiss the congregation, and also to pray over the refreshments in the back. The food smelled good, and it was time to get in line to be served. Michelle went in her wallet; she thought she would have to pay for a plate of food, but that was not so at The Hand of God Ministries. It was free; all of this good food was free.

Everyone fellowshipped in the dining hall and introduced themselves to the visitors. They ate, they laughed, and afterward, everyone cleaned together. Even the Pastor helped clean. Michelle could not believe her eyes; a pastor volunteering to clean was unreal to her. She thought he would be stiff-necked, high minded, proud, and uptight. No, it wasn't like that over at the Hand of God Ministries. After every pot was cleaned, and every crumb was swept up, everyone went home filled. Michelle went home and started going over some of the scriptures that the Pastor had called out during his sermon. She was ready to learn. She was like a babe in Christ, desiring the sincere milk. She studied and prayed, and she went to sleep. Through the week, she had a few obstacles in her way. One of her exes came over, and she fell into temptation. She felt really bad afterward. She was hurt. She let God down, and she let herself down. But God was still standing right there forgiving her and waiting for her to seek him. He loves her. She thought that He would be mad at her. So, she was thinking she may not go to church this Sunday until she can stop giving in to temptation. But there was a voice that said to her, "Come." She got back in her word, and she decided to stay focused this time. It was almost time for Sunday to come back around, and she wanted to be ready and on time. She ironed her clothes, cleaned her house, and put some roast beef in the crockpot. She did not know if they were going to cook this Sunday again, but just in case they did not, she was prepared.

It was Sunday again. She got up out of bed, jumped in the shower and got dressed. She got to church on time, and she sat a little towards the back. She thought she was unworthy to sit close to the front. But the devil is a liar. Before service started, the little lady said, "Everyone, please move closer to the front. Not for me, but for yourself. Thank you." She walked back to her seat and smiled. The congregation knows her sense of humor, and they laughed. She is very silly but serious. She meant what she said, but she said it with love and a smile. Pastor Barney proceeded from the back and service got started. Evangelist Brown got up before they started Praise and Worship. She said, "Anything dead ought to be buried. We came to worship God today. This is a joyful occasion, not a funeral. So, get your hearts and minds clear and off of what went on before you got here, what you are going to eat after service, and what you are going to do this week. We are going to tear the house down praising God today." She took her seat, and the Praise team came up to sing. They sang a few songs, and they sat down. It was testimony service, and there were some powerful testimonies. It was time for Pastor Barney to preach, but he wanted to hear a song from Sister Champagne. She sang a song by Melinda Watts. While she was singing, the congregation was in tears. Not only did her voice sound like an angel, but the words to the song ministered to their hearts. She sang, "No matter what I've done, your love won't turn me away so I will come boldly to your throne of grace."

Pastor Barney got up and said, "God's love will stand. No matter who lets you down, no matter who walks away from you, God's love is everlasting." He then began to pray. After praying before coming forth with the Word, he said, "Today, the topic is Salvation. The only way you can be saved is by believing. Turn with me to Romans 10:9, 10. It says here that if you confess with your mouth the Lord Jesus and shall believe in your heart that God raised him from the dead, you will be saved. For with the heart man believes unto righteousness, and with the mouth confession is made unto salvation." He also preached from the book of Isaiah 55. He said,

"Come, if you are hungry, Come, if you are thirsty. Come to a well that never runs dry. If you want your soul to live, come unto God, this day without hesitation.

No matter what kind of sin you have done, God forgives. He is the forgiver of sins, and he places them into the sea of forgetfulness. He does not remember your sins anymore." Afterward, it was altar call. He said, "If you want salvation, come. God is the only one who can save you, and He is the only one who can complete you." He turned the service over to his wife this time. There were only three people at the altar. Michelle was one of them. The little lady said to her, "Yes, He still loves you, sweetie. Even though you messed up, God is still standing with you. He knows your heart, and this day, you are saved. Go in peace." Michelle went back to her seat with her eyes bucked. She knew that God was the only one who knew that she had slept with someone this week. She knew that it had to be God that gave this little lady the right words to say. Michelle knew that she had found the right church. She knew that she would have to fight harder to stay in the race. The devil was starting to fight her more, bringing more temptation and wicked devices to turn her back to him due to her coming to the Lord. She knows now that she has to stay prayed up and focus on the scriptures and start fasting. It was time for the offering. Deacon Brown was up there this time. He first gave his testimony of how he thought he lost some money but found it in the back pocket of the pants that he washed the day before. He said,

"Isn't God good?" The congregation laughed. They repeated their petition, and they gave their offering. Sister Shantel came with the announcements again, and then Pastor dismissed. He said, "Remember, next Sunday is potluck Sunday. Please be clean while cooking." Everyone laughed. Then he closed out, "May the Lord watch, between me and thee, while we are absent, one from another, Peace," and everyone said, "Likewise." "Tell everyone you love them in Jesus Name, Amen."

Michelle went home with so much joy in her spirit. She prayed and believed God for some things. She wanted to be completely delivered. She asked God to protect her and keep her. The enemy was on an assignment this week. He knew that she was getting too close to God and did not want that to happen. So, he sent John, Demetrius, and Henry her way. She recognized the enemy this time, and she bound everything that was sent her way and cast it back to the pits of hell from whence it came. But she did not know this Troy fellow. He seemed to be okay. But the devil is very deceitful. They talked about God, and he asked for a kiss. She kissed him and shortly realized that this is not of God. She felt bad for kissing him and thought that she let God down once again. "How can I keep failing him?" She asked herself. She thought that she should be perfect by now. She decided to get into her word, and study. She wanted to be delivered, so she studied scriptures concerning deliverance. She stayed up all night reading and praying, and then went to sleep. She believed the scriptures were true, she believed that when she prayed to God, he heard her and answered her. Now it was Saturday. She made pasta salad with grilled chicken inside for the potluck. She got her clothes ready, and she got ready for bed. This time, there was no voice. God knew that she was sincere in her heart and that she wanted Him for sure. She did not need the invitation any longer. She was willing to do this on her own. She no longer needed to be asked.

This Sunday was different. She came in ready, expecting a miracle. She wanted something from God that only God can give. She had salvation and deliverance by faith. She wanted everything God had to offer. She brought God back to the remembrance of His word. She knew the word said, if you knock it will be opened, if you seek you shall find, and if you ask you shall receive. She already had the faith to believe that it shall come to pass. Michelle had joy in her heart. Service started. Evangelist asked Michelle to come forth with a scripture. Michelle was willing but nervous. She has never been in front of the congregation before. When she opened her Bible, it was opened to one of God's promises. She read 2 Chronicles 7:14. She said, "If my people, which are called by my name, shall humble themselves, and pray, and seek my face, and turn from their wicked ways; then will I hear from heaven, and will forgive their sin, and will heal their land." She gave the microphone back to the little lady, and the little lady smiled at her. The little lady said,

"Turn from your wicked ways. Turn from your wicked ways. Humble yourself, pray, and seek; and turn from your wicked ways. No matter how far you have fallen, no matter the situation, no matter how big the problem may be; just come. He wants to heal you and set you free. So, stay humble, seek him while he may be found. Thank you so much, Michelle, for that scripture." It was time for praise and worship service. They sang a song called He's able. They called a young man up by the name of Larry to lead the song. Before they started singing, he said, "Do you know that God will do exceeding abundantly, above all we shall ask or think?" Everyone started to sing the song. The church sang so beautifully together as if they were angels singing to the Lord above.

It was time for the Pastor to come forth with the word. He wanted to hear his wife sing a song. She came up and sang a song called, God of a second chance. After she finished, He preached about deliverance. Michelle was amazed because she was just reading about deliverance this week. It was an assurance from God that she was indeed delivered. She was excited about it. They had an altar call, and everyone was praying on one accord. Michelle started speaking in other tongues, and she praised and worshipped God. While she was still worshipping, the little lady grabbed the microphone and said, "Oh magnify the Lord with me, and let us exalt his name together." Everyone worshipped and praised God.

Michelle was blessed beyond measure that day. There was overflow in the house that Sunday. And every Sunday afterward was more powerful than the one before. Michelle did not know that she was missing the real joy and the peace of God all of her life. She did not know what love felt like until now.

Michelle practiced celibacy and submitted herself to God. She surrendered all to Him. She completely stopped having sex. She became a new creature in Christ. All of the old ways passed away, and everything was new in her life. She was redeemed, and she walked by faith, not by sight. She started attending Sunday school, prayer, and bible study. God took her to higher heights and deeper depths in His word. Intimacy has never been sweeter until now. He invited her in with the word 'come,' and it has been loving ever since.

Chapter 8

Better Seasons

The seasons have changed
The leaves have fallen once again
I've been standing in this space way too long

An entire movement
Have passed me by and
Everyone is moving on with their life

But not I

Haven't moved forward
Don't want to go back
All I hear is the same pitiful words

In my mind there are
Terrible loud noises that
Remind me of my present state

Regret fills my heart and
Shame covers my face
I feel no longer like me

I kept making promises
Said that I would never stay around
Found myself still waiting, waiting for love(lust)

What am I afraid of?
Why am I still here?
Haven't I had enough of your lies

Haven't I cried enough tears
Why is it so hard to walk away?
Why can't I just walk away
Why can't I pick up my feet and just...?
Walk away

Everything's dried up now
Left for dead
No hope left, Just the doubt
Thinking to myself

I've wasted so much time
And of course, I don't blame you
It's my fault for not being strong enough
To have dealings with you
I really thought I was ready
To make grown woman choices
But,
I take responsibility for my weak will and naïve nature

At that time, I did not know
how to be strong, strong enough to walk
I did not recognize your deceit, and I
Am sure you couldn't see yourself either

I asked myself over and over again

Is it too late for me?
Will there be another chance for me?
Will there be a better season for me?

I don't know
but
I embrace all that will come my way
The good and the bad

I do believe that things will get better for me
Due to all of the previous testimonies witnessed before me
I'm sure there is still room for me

I do not believe trouble will last forever
So right now, I make up my mind
To pick up my feet and place
One in front of the other.

I now realize that all
It takes is faith.
I had to believe that I could
Recover from this,
Walk again and move forward into,

My new season

Chapter 9

Thank You

I thought I was strong enough to handle the situations in my life; big and small. But I wasn't as strong as I thought. Life is a lesson. With every lesson, there is a choice to either go through the somethings that life may bring or just give up. With every decision, the consequences may allow us to experience something good or bad. My experiences taught me to be thankful to you. If it were not for you, I wouldn't have gotten through...

Thank You...

For being loved when I hated myself. I couldn't see myself the way you see me. For having respect for me when I did not respect myself. For thinking of me when I didn't think I meant anything to you...

Thank You...

For being strength in my weakness. When I fell short, you always stepped in, grabbed me, and brought me back to the place where I should have stayed.

Thank You...

For being a compass when I was lost. I took so many left turns that the right way seemed so unfamiliar. But God, I thank you for being a Father. I thank you for being strong enough to love a person like me.

You loved me through all my wrong turns, stubborn ways, and all the shortstops.

Thank You...

For being peace when every storm that could come upon me came and would not cease. You are the only one that could calm the thunderous winds around me by saying one word. You spoke 'Peace,' and everything was still. So amazing you are. Who else could speak to a storm, a sea, a raging wind, or an angry rain? Thanks for stepping in right on time. I thought I was over with, I thought I had lost the fight, I almost gave up. But God.

Thank You...

For fighting my battles against every spiritual enemy. In times of trouble, warfare, and chaos; you kept me on every leaning side.

Thank You...

For being favorable towards me. I messed up so many times throughout life. You are so generous to me, so merciful, so sweet, so kind, so faithful, and so patient with me; the sinner. Sometimes I cannot understand your Love for me, nevertheless....

I Thank You, Father!